CHAPTER 1

Elderly Amish widow Ettie Smith stared out the window of the tiny house she shared with her older sister, Elsa-May. "When will the house next door be lived in again? I don't like it being empty. It's not being useful and I like things to fulfil their purpose."

Elsa-May didn't even look up from her knitting. "I wouldn't know."

Ettie gave a wistful sigh. "How I'd love to have some neighbors again."

"Humph. You didn't like the last lot of people who owned the *haus*. You were delighted when they left."

"They were different. I mean some normal people, and you shouldn't say bad things because one of them was killed."

"You can't fool me, Ettie. You want people living there so you can spend the day spying on them."

Ettie's jaw dropped open at the suggestion. "I'd do no such thing. When I see them out the window it's not spying. It's seeing they're okay and that's called being neighborly."

Elsa-May click-clacked her knitting needles together, a sound that often got on Ettie's nerves and she did her best to ignore it. "I hear Gabriel is looking for someone to move in and lease it from him."

"Why didn't you tell me?" Ettie asked.

"I'm telling you now. I'll believe it when it happens because he's been saying that for months. It would be good if he does something about it, then he wouldn't have to keep the grass cut and clean the *haus* all the time. It's a lot of work and the place must be costing him money with the taxes and whatever else."

Ettie huffed. "When do you talk to him without me?"

"I couldn't tell you. Anyway, are we ready to leave?"

Ettie looked over at the clock that sat atop the mantle. "It's not time yet. You said half an hour after nine and it's only nine."

"Just checking that you'll be ready to leave on time."

"Jah, I will."

Elsa-May smiled. "I just love quilting bees, don't you?"

From her seat on the couch, Ettie tied her *kapp* strings under her chin. *"Jah."*

Elsa-May stared at her sister. "You don't sound enthusiastic."

"I am. I said I like them, and I do."

Elsa-May put her knitting in the bag under her chair and then sat with her hands clasped in her lap. Ettie knew she was about to get picked on.

"One thing I've noticed about you, Ettie—"

"Please don't start on me so early. The day has barely begun. Wait at least until after lunch, would you?"

Elsa-May took off her knitting glasses and looped them over the front of her dress. "All I was going to say is you're not happy unless you're doing something that you suggest. I joined us up to the quilting bee and now you act as though I'm dragging you along by your left ear."

"I'm happy to go."

"But if it'd been your idea you'd be excited for it."

Ettie pushed herself to her feet. There was no way to win this one. "I'll tidy the kitchen." Ettie had to get away from Elsa-May before they had another argument. It was much nicer in the house when they were talking to one another. All Elsa-May did these days was criticize and when Ettie didn't agree with her, Elsa-May had taken to giving her the silent treatment. It was either that or her hearing was getting even worse. Or was it, perhaps, a case of selective deafness?

"I'll take Snowy for a quick walk," Elsa-May said, just as Ettie was about to step into the kitchen.

"There's no time for that."

"I said a quick one. We'll only be gone ten minutes."

"Okay." Ettie walked into the kitchen muttering under her breath, "That's ten minutes of peace I'll get."

"What was that, Ettie?" Elsa-May called out.

"The kitchen's a mess." Ettie's shock over her sister hearing her softly spoken words was replaced with annoyance over how the kitchen had been left.

"Just as well you're cleaning it then. I thought I'd be left with it again."

Was she kidding? Ettie marched out of the kitchen to confront her sister and saw Elsa-May standing there staring at her with hands on her hips. "You've got your puzzle spread all over the kitchen table from last night. You said you'd clear it away as soon as we finished breakfast. What am I supposed to do with it?"

"Don't you touch one piece. It'll be finished in a day or two."

"That long?"

"I'm getting it done way ahead of the recommended time. The package said suitable for over ten years and I'll be finished with it tomorrow." Elsa-May chuckled at her own joke, and that made Ettie forget her urge to have the kitchen ordered and spotless. "Let's go, Snowy." Snowy scampered over to Elsa-May wagging his tail.

When Elsa-May and Snowy left, Ettie walked back into the kitchen shaking her head. "Peace and quiet at

last." She grabbed the puzzle box and saw on the side that it said recommended for over ten years. Ettie put her hand over her mouth and laughed. She wasn't certain whether her sister was having a joke with her or if she meant it. Anything was possible.

Deena Brown, one of the ladies in the community, had given Elsa-May the puzzle, telling her it was for when the day came she could no longer knit. Elsa-May didn't wait for that day to come before she began the puzzle.

On looking around the kitchen again, Ettie saw it wasn't so bad. It was just that the puzzle made the place look untidy. The breakfast washing up had already been done, the dishes put away, but Ettie found two crumbs on the countertop. She skittered them into the sink with a damp cloth.

"Quilting bee," Ettie grumbled, wiping her hands on her apron. "I suppose it will be fun, but only if Elsa-May is sitting on the opposite side of the room."

NOT LONG AFTER Elsa-May and Snowy finished their walk, Annie Lapp arrived at their house in her horse and buggy to pick them up. Annie was hosting the quilting bee at her house.

Once the ladies were outside the house, Elsa-May pushed past Ettie to sit in the front seat, so Ettie sat in the back—as usual.

Before Ettie could close the door, a black cat pounced on her, and she let out a yelp. "What's this?"

Elsa-May turned around and she was confronted by a smoky colored cat that leaped on her lap from the floor, causing her also to let out a yell.

"Quick, close the doors!" Annie ordered.

Both women did as she said.

"You have cats in your buggy?" Elsa-May patted the cat that was purring loudly on her lap.

"Only the two. I don't let them out of the *haus* anymore, but I do bring them for a ride in the buggy when I can."

"That's interesting," Elsa-May said, as the large black cat moved from Ettie's lap to sit on her lap. The smoky cat changed places, too, moving into the back seat to sit on Ettie.

Ettie patted him, admiring his long white whiskers. "Such nice markings on this one. One white paw and a large white marking on his chest that looks like a bib."

Annie moved her horse and buggy onward.

"Why do you bring them in the buggy, Annie?" Elsa-May asked.

"Just to give them a change. Something exciting in their day. I tried to take them for a walk once, but neither of them liked the collar or the lead."

"I've never known anyone to walk a cat."

"Ah, but people do, Elsa-May, people do. Pepper and Smokie like it when we have visitors, but I'm afraid that when I'm sewing I need to lock them in their

A PUZZLING AMISH MURDER

BOOK 23 ETTIE SMITH AMISH MYSTERY

SAMANTHA PRICE

bedroom. They try to attack the thread, and once they got themselves into a terrible tangle. I had to cut them both out of a web of thread and I wasted yards of it. It was the expensive kind, too."

Elsa-May pushed the cat onto the floor of the buggy. "Did you say they have a bedroom?"

"They do."

Ettie gasped. "One each?"

Annie glanced over at Ettie in the backseat. *"Nee.* That would be weird." Annie turned back to the road. "They like to share."

"Of course they do," Ettie muttered.

"They keep me company. Much like you two keep each other company. Luke and I weren't blessed with *kinner* and I have no *schweschder* to share my life with. They've all gone home to *Gott* now, as you know. I've been alone for weeks now with Luke helping out his cousin in Ohio, so the kitties keep me company."

Ettie felt sorry for her loneliness. "When is he coming back?"

"He was supposed to be here already, but he's always running late. He said he'll be a few more days."

When Annie arrived at her home, she said, "Don't open the doors just yet. The other guests will be arriving soon. Maybe one of them can drive you both home?"

"I'd say they will, but should we stay for the quilting bee first?"

Annie frowned at Elsa-May.

"Elsa-May's joking," Ettie explained.

Annie laughed. "You with your funny comments, Elsa-May. Of course you'll stay for the quilting bee and then we'll find someone to take you home. All the ladies are coming except for Deena Brown."

Ettie leaned toward the front. "Is she ill?"

"She didn't say. I found a note at my door this morning saying she wouldn't be able to make it. No reason why, just a short note. It was odd, but I'm not going to judge her for rudeness. At least she was caring enough to inform me."

Ettie asked, "Why didn't she knock on the door and tell you herself?"

Elsa-May shielded her face again from the cat as it jumped up again and was now smoothing his back around her neck. "Perhaps she was too early and thought you might be asleep."

"You might be right, Elsa-May. *Jah,* that must be it."

Elsa-May suggested, "Why don't you go inside with the cats, Annie, and Ettie and I can unhitch the buggy for you?"

"Are you sure?"

"I am."

"*Wunderbaar, denke.* Just put the horse in that paddock." She nodded to the only paddock that adjoined the barn.

"We will."

When Annie was inside with her feline friends, Ettie noticed there was another buggy horse in the paddock. Two horses were a lot of work for an elderly woman like Annie. "I feel sorry for poor Annie doing everything herself while Luke's away."

"It can't be easy, but there are a few women in the community who live alone permanently, so it's harder for them."

Now Ettie was a little grateful to have her sister's company, no matter how irritating she was at times.

Once they got the buggy unhitched and rubbed the horse down, Ettie led the horse toward the paddock. "Open the gate will you, Elsa-May?"

Elsa-May lifted up her long dress and hurried forward.

Ettie brought the horse through to the center of the paddock and then unbuckled his headgear. "Off you go, boy." Ettie patted his neck. Just when she was about to head back to Elsa-May who was waiting at the gate, Ettie smelled something awful.

"Come on. I can't stand here all day, Ettie. What are you doing looking up at the sky like that? Are you bird watching, or what?" Elsa-May looked upward.

"I'm not looking, I'm smelling."

Frowning, Elsa-May looked around and her nose twitched disapprovingly. "Horse manure. Before we go, we'll rake the paddock for her."

Ettie bit her lip. "It's not that."

"Jah, it is." Elsa-May pointed at a pile and tsk tsked. "There's a big mound of it over there. She should be

spreading it over her garden, not piling it up in one corner like that."

"It's not manure that's bothering me. To me, horse manure never smells bad, but something around here does and I don't like it." Ettie tilted her head to catch the breeze. If the breeze was coming from the direction of the trees, then that was the direction of the smell. Ettie walked out the gate and while Elsa-May moved through and put the latch over it, Ettie kept walking.

"Ettie, the *haus* is this way. What are you doing?"

Ettie was too focused to acknowledge her sister, and with every step she took, the odor got stronger.

There was no mistaking the sweet sickly scent, but she hoped and prayed that her suspicions were wrong.

Then she spotted a dog, digging. Knowing the dog didn't belong to Annie, she hurried forward, clapping her hands to scare him away. "Shoo! Get out of there!"

The dog looked up at her, grabbed something and ran off. Ettie squinted at what was in the dog's mouth as the animal ran down the road.

It was a shoe!

A few steps later, she looked down and saw she was right.

And, so was Annie about Deena not coming to the quilting bee… because Deena was dead.

CHAPTER 2

Elsa-May rushed to Ettie's side. "Oh no, Ettie. Is she?"

Ettie didn't even look at her sister. It was obvious the woman was dead and had been for some days. She was half covered in dirt, having been uncovered by the dog. "She is. We'll have to call the police."

"We'll need to cover her with something. The ladies will be arriving soon and we don't want them to see her like this."

"I'll grab something out of the barn."

"I'll tell Annie what's going on."

The two sisters went their separate ways.

In the barn, Ettie found a horse blanket. She knew the detective might be upset if the blanket disturbed what he would call the 'crime scene,' but she didn't have a choice. No one should see Deena in that state.

Ettie tried not to look as she lowered the blanket over Deena's body. "Sorry about that, Deena."

Ettie then put some large stones on the four corners of the horse blanket, so it wouldn't blow around in a gust of wind. After that, she dusted off her hands and headed to the phone in Annie's barn to make the call to the police.

After Elsa-May broke the news to Annie, she then had the job of standing at the gate to turn away all the ladies coming for the quilting bee.

One by one they arrived and Elsa-May told them the quilting bee was canceled because a body was found. She didn't think it right to tell them who it was before the authorities got there, and before the loved ones were informed.

Once Ettie notified the police, the second call she made was to their Amish bishop, Paul. Mary, his wife, had taken the call as the bishop wasn't home. Mary was now busy looking for a phone number or address for Deena's relatives.

Ettie then went to the house and saw Annie in a dreadful state. She sat down with her in the kitchen comforting her as she cried into a white handkerchief.

"She must've died today after she left the note for me this morning," Annie said.

Ettie knew that wasn't right. The woman had been dead for days. "You say she left a note today?"

"*Jah,* that's right. Do you want to see it?"

Ettie knew she'd get into terrible trouble if she

touched something that would later become evidence. "*Nee*, but the police will want to see it."

"I don't want them here. They have no right." Annie got up and reached for a piece of paper on the countertop.

"Don't touch it," Ettie said, as she hurried forward. "If that's the note, you can't touch it."

"Why not?"

"The police will want to do some testing on it—fingerprints and such. It is possible that her death might not have been an accident."

"What? Do you think someone killed her?"

Ettie shrugged her shoulders, fearing a bad reaction. "It's possible."

Annie cried some more. "I don't want the police here and I don't want them looking at the last thing poor old Deena wrote. I should throw it away. I don't want any trouble. I'll not mention it to them and neither should you." Annie peered at Ettie.

Ettie frowned and looked down at the note. "I can't forget about it. I know it's here and I've seen it now, too."

Ettie read the note.

I'm sorry Annie, but it is impossible for me to make it to the quilting bee today. I am going away for a few weeks to visit an old family friend. I'll come see you when I get back.

Deena.

Ettie bit her lip. "She didn't say who she was visiting."

"No, but she didn't get there."

While Annie sniffed and patted her eyes with the handkerchief, Ettie looked around at the pale-yellow kitchen. Everything was yellow, from the curtains that covered the window above the sink, to the cupboards, the walls, the flooring. Even the plastic tablecloth was yellow. There was no need to guess what Annie's favorite color was.

At the back door were two food plates and two bowls of water for the cats. Ettie was surprised the cats didn't eat at the table with Annie. Perhaps they did when Annie didn't have visitors.

"I honestly can't believe this has happened, Ettie. And why did *Gott* allow her to die so close to my *haus?* Why not somewhere else? Why not at your *haus?"*

Just as Ettie was thinking of an answer, she heard cars. She rose to her feet, moved the yellow curtain aside and saw Kelly's white car along with two police cars. She'd never been happier to see Detective Kelly. "It's the police."

"Wayne will be devastated. He loved her, he did."

Ettie turned around. "Wayne Stoltzfus?"

"Jah, and he wasn't her only admirer. Wayne wanted to marry her, but she wasn't keen. Now, they'll never be married unless people marry in the Lord's *haus.* That will be little comfort to Wayne because he's still alive." Annie stood up and joined Ettie, following her gaze out the window. "Look at all those police."

"And that's Detective Kelly who's just getting out of

the white car. I know him." She let go of the curtains and looked back at Annie. "Will you be all right for a minute, here by yourself? I should talk to the detective. Elsa-May won't want to talk with him alone."

"I'll be fine. I'll check on my kitties. I won't let them out of the bedroom until everyone leaves. They might be frightened by the noise of the cars and all the people."

"Okay." As soon as Annie was in the cats' bedroom, Ettie walked out of the house to join Elsa-May at the gate. As Ettie walked, she tried to recall if she'd ever seen Wayne and Deena together, and she couldn't.

Just as Ettie reached her sister, Kelly looked up at them and walked over.

CHAPTER 3

"Well, well, well. Mrs. Smith and Mrs. Lutz. I wasn't surprised to get your call this morning, Mrs. Smith. It's been too quiet. I knew it wouldn't last for long. No rest for the wicked, as they say." He chuckled. "I'd only just finished my second coffee and was about to start on a mountain of paperwork. You saved me from having to do it, for the moment."

"It's a pity Deena couldn't have been saved," Elsa-May said.

Kelly looked over at the uniformed police and the evidence collecting team in their white coverall suits. They had just arrived in a large white van. Then another car approached. "That's the coroner. Wait here; don't go anywhere. I have to talk with the both of you. But first, I need to see what his initial impressions are."

Ettie and Elsa-May stood together in the middle of the driveway. "How's Annie?" Elsa-May asked.

"She's rattled and upset. I saw the note Deena left. Well, we know Deena didn't write it. Someone's playing games."

"It sounds like it. Why would Deena be there under that tree?"

Ettie said, "She was half buried. I'd dare say she was fully buried before that white dog dug her up."

"The dog ran away with the shoe, didn't it?"

Ettie nodded.

"If you're positive you saw a dog, you should tell Kelly about that."

"I was going to, but he left too quickly."

"You stay here and tell Kelly everything. I'll go in and look after Annie. The poor thing's had a terrible fright."

"So have I. I was the one who found Deena."

"You're used to this kind of thing, Annie is not." With that, Elsa-May turned on her heel and left Ettie standing in the middle of the driveway, alone, to face Detective Kelly when he came back.

"Okay," Ettie called after her. "Just don't scare the cats."

Elsa-May stopped and turned around. "They better watch that they don't scare me."

Once Ettie saw that Elsa-May was in the house, she wandered over to the paddock and leaned against the fence. From there, she had a clear view of what was going on. Two cars drove by slowly, and then they stopped and people got out to see what was happening. A police officer moved them along, while another officer fixed yellow crime scene tape around the trees that surrounded the body.

Eventually, Kelly wandered back over to Ettie, pulling out a notepad and pen from his inner coat pocket. "Mrs. Smith, what time did you arrive here today?"

"I'm not certain exactly, but I can tell you Annie picked us up in her buggy for the quilting bee at nine thirty. That's when she got to our house. You see, it was to be held here today."

"The quilting bee?"

"Yes."

"At nine thirty?"

"That's the time we left our house, so the actual quilting bee was due to start later."

"I see." He looked at his watch and then made a couple of notes.

Ettie took a step toward him and looked up into his face. "Deena left a note on Annie's door saying she wouldn't be here today, but it couldn't have come from her because she was already dead. She had to have been dead, already. I saw the body. She's been dead for days, wouldn't you think so?"

"I agree." He pursed his lips. "Dead people can't write notes. I'll take a closer look at it."

"I thought you'd want to take a look. Maybe take the note in as evidence so the experts can examine it."

He frowned at her. "So the dead woman was...?"

"Deena Brown."

"D-E-A-N-A—"

"No, it's D-E-E-N-A, and her last name is just like the color, B-R-O-W-N."

"Deena Brown," he repeated as he jotted it down in his notebook. "And are you positive she was supposed to be here today for the quilting bee?"

"Yes. As far as I know."

"And the owner of the house here got a note from Deena saying she wouldn't be attending?"

Ettie nodded. "The note was signed "Deena," but it couldn't have been from her. Not unless she wrote it days ago. If she wrote it days ago, why was it placed here this morning? And, by whom was it placed?"

He slowly nodded. "I agree with you about that. I don't need the coroner to tell me she didn't die within the last twenty-four hours. It's obvious she's been dead for days."

"And, I saw a dog running off with her shoe. I think it was her shoe. It must've been."

His eyebrows rose. "A dog, you say?"

"A white one. Medium sized, and skinny with long legs. It looked like a hound dog."

He looked behind him. "Which way did the dog go?"

"He ran down the road that way." She flung her arm out to the left.

"Stay here."

He walked away and talked to another plainclothes detective. When he returned, he asked for Deena's address, and inquired about Deena's family members.

"I can tell you where she lives, I mean, where she *lived,* but I don't know about her family. Her husband is Hezekiah Lapp, but he disappeared around ten years ago and no one knows where he went. Some say he died, but I think that's a rumor."

"Interesting. Hezekiah Lapp," Kelly said as he jotted that down. "Not Hezekiah Brown?"

"That's right. I remember she had a son, but I don't think anyone's seen him for years, either. She was on her own. I also called our bishop, right after calling you, and his wife is looking for a phone number or address for any of Deena's relatives. There is a man who is rumored to be in love with her, Wayne Stoltzfus. Annie might know more about that situation."

"And she lived alone now that both her son and her husband have vanished?"

Ettie frowned. "Yes, but her son didn't just vanish like the husband did. He left the community. It was the husband who left suddenly with no explanation, not a word, and no one's seen or heard from him since."

"I'll have the team comb through Deena's house when they finish up here." He nodded toward Annie's house. "I'll talk with Annie next. I take it she's home?"

"That's right."

"Thank you. And, do you know where I can find Wayne Stoltzfus?"

"His farm is about two miles up this road. It's a large white house and it's close to the road. The same direction the dog went."

He jotted that down. "Tell me about this quilting bee. Was it just the four of you who were planning on attending? The two of you, Deena and Annie? No one else is here?"

"There would've been others, but we had to turn the ladies away. After we found poor Deena, Elsa-May had to tell the ladies to go home because we found a body and we were waiting for the police. I told her not to tell anyone it was Deena. The only person who knows is Annie and, of course, the bishop's wife. And probably the bishop too by now."

Kelly rubbed his chin. "I'll speak with Annie now and see what she can tell me." He started walking toward the house again and Ettie followed.

When they got closer, Ettie moved in front of him and opened the door. "Hello," Ettie called out.

"Come in," Annie said from somewhere within the house.

They found Elsa-May and Annie sitting at the kitchen table.

"Annie, this is Detective Kelly."

Annie stood up and nodded. "Nice to meet you. I'm Annie Lapp."

"Nice to meet you, Mrs. Lapp. Thank you for speaking with me."

"Ettie said it would be okay, so I trust her."

Elsa-May stood up. "Would you like us to leave, detective, so you can talk without us here?"

"Please stay!" Annie grabbed hold of Elsa-May's sleeve.

CHAPTER 4

The detective glared at Elsa-May. "You can stay as long as you don't answer the questions I ask Mrs. Lapp."

Elsa-May sat down again and Kelly stared from one sister to the other until they agreed to keep quiet.

"Please sit," Annie said to the detective.

Kelly sat down and then opened his notebook and readied his pen. "Mrs. Lapp, is there a Mr. Lapp?"

"Why?"

"Just wondering if you live alone or…"

"My husband is late."

Detective Kelly frowned. "I'm sorry about that. It can't be easy being left on your own."

"He's coming back soon."

Kelly's eyebrows rose.

Ettie saw what was going on. "Excuse me. Annie's

husband is away. He's still alive. He's late because he should've been back from Ohio by now."

"Oh, he's still alive, Mrs. Lapp?"

"Very much so. I never said he was dead. He's helping out a friend. He'll come home as soon as he hears. I must let him know."

"When was the last time you saw Deena?"

Annie looked up at the ceiling. "It must be several days ago."

"So, several meaning twelve?"

"No. A few days. Maybe five or six, possibly. I wouldn't like to say because I don't want to tell a fib."

"Yet you thought Deena was coming here today?"

"I went to her house to see if she was coming because she wasn't at the Sunday meeting. She could've been sick. That's what I thought, and I was worried about her."

"Right. So that was the last time you saw her?"

Annie shook her head. "No. She wasn't there, or if she was there, she didn't come to the door. I thought I heard a noise coming from inside the house. I left her a note. I took a note with me in case she wasn't home. I always like to be prepared for every eventuality."

"But, she might've been sick. Didn't you go inside to check that she was okay?" Elsa-May asked, earning a glare from Kelly.

"No, I didn't. Deena and I didn't always get along. Well, we did, and then we didn't. She was moody. I'd almost say she was unpredictable. I thought she might not have wanted to talk with me."

"Is that so?" Detective Kelly raised his eyebrows. "Mrs. Smith told me that the two of you were close."

"We were at times. The friendship was a one-sided thing. Sometimes she was friendly, and at other times she wasn't. It would leave me thinking I might've done something to unknowingly upset her. Then a few days would pass and everything would be back to normal. It was an up and down friendship."

Ettie nodded, thinking of her sister. "I know exactly what you mean."

Detective Kelly frowned at her. "Please, Mrs. Smith, you promised."

"It was only a comment. I didn't answer a question."

"Please let Mrs. Lapp do the talking." Detective Kelly looked back at Annie. "Now, back to the day you were at her house. Tell me about that."

"I don't want you to think that she wasn't a nice person because she was. Maybe I'm too sensitive." Annie nervously tugged at the neckline of her dark blue dress.

"I understand. What happened that last time you went to her house?" Kelly asked once more.

"I didn't think it odd that she didn't answer the door because she was sometimes funny like that, so I left a note for her inviting her here today. That's all I can tell you."

Kelly jotted some things down. Then he looked up at Annie once more. "And why did you continue the friendship with Deena, Mrs. Lapp? Given the odd nature of the friendship?"

"Some people are like that, I told myself. Some are easier to get along with than others. Seeing she didn't have many women friends, I tried very hard to be one for her."

"There was never any argument or disagreement over anything?" Kelly asked.

"No. I was trying to make an effort with her. I don't like leaving people out of things, and I didn't want her to feel that no one liked her. That's why I went there to invite her."

"You say she didn't have many women friends, so did she have men friends?"

"She often talked with Wayne Stoltzfus."

"Wayne Stoltzfus, yes, Mrs. Smith told me where he lives. I'll be speaking with him soon."

"He'll be so upset." Annie shook her head, looking down.

"Can I see the note she left you?" Kelly asked.

"Yes." Annie stood and headed to the kitchen.

"Don't touch it, please." He bounded to his feet and followed her.

"I touched it earlier."

"Please don't touch it again." He leaned down to read it. "And is that her handwriting?"

"Yes, she wrote it. It says her name right there at the bottom."

"It can't be if it was written today. Deena has been dead for a few days."

She gasped and covered her mouth. "She has been dead outside my house for days?"

"I'm sorry to deliver the news, but that's the way things are pointing at the moment. I won't know more until I get a full report."

Annie held her hand against her chest. "A car has most likely run her down. They always speed along these straight roads between the fields."

"That might explain her being dead but not about her being buried," The words slipped out of Ettie's mouth before she could stop them. "I'm sorry," she said to Kelly, covering her mouth with her hand.

Annie's face screwed up. "She was buried out there? No, that can't be right." Now Annie was more distressed.

Ettie could feel Elsa-May's disapproval while Kelly shot her a look of disdain.

"As I said, we won't know anything for certain until the reports come in. Meanwhile, I'll need this letter."

Annie looked down at the letter. "Do you have to?"

"Yes. It is a murder investigation and it could provide valuable clues."

"No. I don't want you to have it."

Kelly tilted his head to one side. "Are you hiding something from me, Mrs. Lapp?"

"No. I'm not. Okay, take the note. It was my last thing from Deena, that's why I want to keep it. Can I have it back when you're done with it?"

"It's unlikely. It's a key piece of evidence and hopefully we'll find who did this to her and if we don't have a confession, this could be the evidence that might get us a conviction." Without saying another word, Kelly reached into his pocket and pulled out a large plastic bag. "Do you have kitchen tongs?"

"I do. I keep them for turning the meat over when I'm cooking. I used to use a fork but then I got splashed with sizzling hot fat. Tongs allow me to be further away."

Kelly didn't comment, but Ettie knew if she had said that, Kelly would've told them he didn't need a cooking lesson.

Annie opened one of the yellow drawers beside her kitchen sink and handed him a pair of tongs.

Kelly opened the plastic bag, used the tongs to pick up the document, slipped it into the bag and then ziplocked it closed. "Thank you." He handed back the tongs.

"What happens now?" Annie closed the tongs back in the drawer.

"I'll need to know where I can find her relatives before they find out from other people."

"I don't know where..."

Elsa-May said, "She had a son and only one. His

name's Ryker. I'll contact Bishop Paul. If anyone has a way to contact him it'll be the bishop."

"I've already done that," Ettie told her. "He was out when I called just now. I spoke to Mary and she's looking for a phone number or address for Ryker."

"I do hope Bishop Paul will tell Wayne before anyone else. This will destroy him."

Kelly pulled his cell phone out of his pocket. "One of you ladies can step outside and call the bishop's wife again. She might've found out something by now."

"I'll do it," said Ettie. Kelly gave her a pen and a slip of paper ripped from his notebook. It surprised Ettie that Kelly didn't trust her with his book.

She took the phone outside, and made a call to the phone that Bishop Paul had inside his barn.

As soon as Mary answered, Ettie blurted out, "Mary, have you found out anything?"

"Ettie?"

"*Jah,* it's me again."

"Do you have a pen?" Mary asked.

"I do."

Mary gave her Ryker Lapp's phone number.

"Is that all? No other relatives?"

"*Nee,* just the son and I don't have his address. It's my fault. I'm in charge of this kind of thing. I'll need to look at updating all our records."

"*Denke* for that. One more thing, Mary. I have heard that Wayne Stoltzfus was a friend of Deena's."

"It's true, they were close. Paul's gone there to tell him now."

"That's nice to know. I'll tell Annie. She was worried about him and how he'd find out."

"We were too."

Ettie ended the call and headed back into the house.

"Here's a phone number for the son," Ettie announced when she walked back into the kitchen. "And that's his number there, but there is no other way to contact him." She handed Kelly his phone along with the slip of paper.

"Ryker Lapp." He looked up at Annie. "Lapp is your last name. Wasn't the deceased's last name Brown?"

"Did I forget to say that both our husbands are brothers?" Annie asked.

Ettie told the detective, "Deena went back to her maiden name after her husband disappeared. Before that, she was also a Lapp. Ryker left us years ago when he was a very young man."

Elsa-May said, "I've already told the detective that, Ettie."

"I know. I never said you didn't."

Kelly ignored them and stared at Annie, seeming a little bothered. "Ryker Lapp is your nephew?"

"Yes, but only by marriage. He's my late husband's step-nephew."

Kelly's lips turned down at the corners while he shook his head slightly.

Elsa-May put her hand lightly on Annie's arm.

"Annie, stop calling Luke your late husband. It makes him sound like... well it makes you sound like you're a widow."

Annie covered her mouth. "I didn't mean it like that, but he *is* late."

"Just call him Luke or your husband," Ettie suggested.

Annie nodded.

Kelly continued, "And do you know where I might find your step-nephew?"

"No. Or I would've said so at the start. Just because he's my step-nephew by marriage doesn't mean I kept in touch."

"How old is he?"

"Maybe in his early twenties by now."

"And Deena would've been...?"

"About forty, fifty, or even sixty. I didn't ask and I don't remember her ever saying."

"I have written down his phone number," Ettie said. "You can call him."

Kelly turned to face Ettie, and snapped, "Thanks for your permission, Mrs. Smith, I will."

Ettie pressed her lips together. He didn't have to be sarcastic. "Also, the bishop has gone to inform Wayne Stoltzfus of what's happened."

"Very well. I'll need to ask Mr. Stoltzfus some questions." Then they all heard scratching. Kelly looked around. "What's that?"

"That's Pepper and Smokie. They're trying to get

out. They like to meet visitors if there are only a few. They don't like it when I have a houseful of people, but they love visitors if there are only one or two of them. Would you like to meet them, Detective Kelly?"

Ettie leaned forward and told him, "They're cats."

He grimaced. "The way my day's been going, they'd have to be black cats."

A smile lit up Annie's face. "They're mostly black. How did you know?"

He breathed out heavily. "A wild guess. It fits completely."

Annie stood up. "I'll let them out."

"No! Please don't. I have allergies." Kelly rubbed his arms.

"That's unfortunate."

"Yes." He took a step backward. "It is. Thank you for your time and your cooperation, Mrs. Lapp. I'll be in touch soon."

"I'm willing to help all I can. I'd love to find out why she died here on my property. Perhaps she died after she left the note when she was hurrying away so I wouldn't see her."

Ettie was amazed that Annie wasn't fully taking in that Deena couldn't have written the note.

Kelly looked at Annie, and Ettie could see he didn't want to have to tell her again. All he said was, "We'll find out soon enough."

"You will let me know, won't you? I'll feel so guilty if she died by tripping over a fallen tree branch or something like that. Or, a root of the tree sticking up from the ground. You know how they do that? Not all roots stay under the ground like they're meant to."

"I'll walk out with you," Ettie said to Detective Kelly.

Once they were clear of the house, Kelly asked, "What do you know about any of this?"

"Nothing. Elsa-May and I weren't that close with Deena, but she did give Elsa-May a jigsaw puzzle a few weeks ago." Ettie looked over at the men in white suits combing the surrounding area. There were now fewer onlookers, but a reporter had arrived with a photographer. "I hope people won't knock on Annie's door and bother her."

"We can put tape across her driveway when we leave. I can also have a patrol car keep an eye on her house over the next couple of days. Is there anyone she can stay with?"

"Not us. You've seen how small our house is. It's barely big enough for the two of us. And we can hardly take in her cats, what with Snowy. If you think she should stay somewhere, she could stay with the bishop and his wife."

He looked at his watch. "See how she feels. If she's nervous, she should stay elsewhere."

Ettie tugged on her prayer *kapp* strings. She'd rather him say one way or the other. "Does it look like Deena's been murdered?"

He stared down his nose at Ettie. "The woman was buried."

Ettie felt like a fool. "She was, too. Oh dear."

"There is a chance it was an accidental death somehow, and then someone covered it up. She might've been hit by a car. The driver stopped and got out, when they saw her dead, they buried her."

"Are you trying to make me feel better? There's not much chance that happened. Why wouldn't they just drive off? And, why was she on foot so far from home? It's two miles away. I suppose she could've walked."

"That's my next stop, her home. I'll do that before I talk to the deceased's boyfriend."

"He wasn't her boyfriend. She was a married woman, so better to call him a friend since no one knows where Hezekiah is." Ettie pulled her mouth to one side wishing she could take a look around Deena's home with Kelly, but he would never allow it. "I hope you can find out who did this."

"I will get to the bottom of it."

"Is there anything you'd like Elsa-May and me to do?"

"Yes."

Ettie smiled, delighted to be of some help.

"You can keep out of my way, and see to it that Mrs. Lapp is all right. It would've been a nasty shock, being a part-time friend of the victim." He grinned.

Ettie didn't find what he said funny and didn't know why he was smiling so much lately. He wasn't normally someone who smiled. "I was the one who found her. Don't you think it was a shock for me?"

"You're used to it."

Ettie's lips closed tightly. That was the same thing Elsa-May had said to her.

"If you find anything out," Kelly said, "you have my number."

"I do." She tapped her head. "It's in here."

He smiled again and gave her a nod. "Good day, Mrs. Smith."

"Bye." Ettie walked back to the house and joined Annie and Elsa-May who were looking out the window.

Ettie sat on one of the two couches.

"What did he say?" Annie asked Ettie.

"He said if you don't feel comfortable here you should stay with someone else for a while. I thought you might be able to stay with Bishop Paul and Mary."

"*Ach nee*. I won't be able to take my cats if I go there. I just have to hope and pray that Luke will be home soon."

"They'll be okay here for a day or two if you leave food and water out for them," Elsa-May said. "Do you have the dry pellets—kibble?"

"*Nee,* I can't do that. They'll be wandering around worried where I am and why I'm not home. I couldn't do it. No, I won't. I'm not scared of anything. *Gott* will protect me. We'll be all right. I'll lock my doors and my windows."

"We'll check on you as often as we can," Elsa-May said.

"So, it sounds like she was killed," Annie said.

"They think so, but it might be possible it was an accident."

"When will they know?"

Ettie shrugged her shoulders. "In a few hours. Possibly not until tomorrow."

Annie looked over at the boxes in the corner that were brimming with quilting supplies. "The quilting bee will have to wait until all this is over. I won't rest easy until they find out what happened to her." She looked down at the brown rug that filled the middle of the living room. "I might take a nap."

Ettie knew Annie wouldn't be able to sleep, but it was her way of saying she wanted to be alone. "That's an idea." Ettie pushed herself to her feet.

"How are you two getting home?" Annie asked.

"I forgot about that. We have no way to get home."

"I'll take you."

"Nee, Annie. You'll stay and rest. It's either a taxi, or..." Ettie moved to the window and saw Kelly was still outside. "We might ask the detective if he can arrange for someone to drive us home."

"He's not running a taxi service, Ettie," Elsa-May said.

"Still, he's done it before."

Elsa-May stood. "Let's hurry so you can ask him before he leaves."

"Will you be okay, Annie?" Ettie asked.

"I will. If I feel I have to, I'll go to Mary's *haus*."

"Good."

After they said goodbye, Ettie and Elsa-May hurried over to Detective Kelly. They stood a few feet away while he finished giving instructions to an officer. Then he looked up at them. "Hello again. What can I do for you?"

"Would you have someone who could drive us home?" Ettie braced herself for a sarcastic response before he agreed to get one of the officers to do it. That's what he'd normally do—make them squirm, and then be nice.

"I can take you home if you can wait five minutes."

"We can wait." Ettie grabbed Elsa-May's arm and together they walked a few steps back.

"Surely no one would've killed Deena," Elsa-May hissed.

"Something fishy is going on. Why was the note left on Annie's doorstep? Someone was covering up her death. Also, it had to have been someone who knew that Deena was expected here today."

Elsa-May tapped on her chin. "Who could Deena have upset?"

"I don't know. We'll have to ask around."

"Okay, ladies. Are you ready?" Kelly clapped his hands. "The car's this way."

The sisters followed Kelly to the car and then he opened the doors for them.

"You sit in the front, Elsa-May," Ettie said, as she slid into the back seat.

He closed the doors, and then took his time in walking around the car and opening the driver's door. "Buckle up," he told them, as he slid into the driver's seat.

"Done already," Ettie said.

"Me as well," Elsa-May added.

Detective Kelly started the engine and then pulled the car onto the road.

CHAPTER 5

"What did the coroner say?" Elsa-May asked.

Kelly took his eyes off the road and glanced at her. "She has a head injury and at this stage that seems to be the cause of death. He estimated her to have been dead four to five days. I'll know more tomorrow, or maybe tonight when he's had time for a more thorough examination of the body."

Ettie didn't like Deena being referred to as 'the body' or 'the deceased.' A week ago, she was a living, breathing human being.

"You must be able to tell me something about Deena Brown. What was she like?" he asked.

"She lived alone. She was a widow, and her son left the community."

"Elsa-May, she wasn't a widow, remember? Not that anyone knows, anyway. Hezekiah disappeared."

"I meant for all intents and purposes she was like a widow."

Ettie shook her head. Why couldn't her sister just admit when she was wrong?

"I'm intrigued. Tell me about his disappearance."

"Everything seemed fine and then one day he was gone. It broke both their hearts—the boy and Deena."

"He just vanished?"

"Yes."

"How long ago?"

"Over ten years ago."

"Did they file a missing person's report?"

The sisters looked at each other. "We've got no idea," Elsa-May told him.

"I'll look it up on the system and I'll see what I can find out. Do things just happen like that within your community?"

"No!" Ettie said.

"What about Deena herself, what was she like?"

Ettie looked at her sister. "What would you say, Elsa-May?"

"Very friendly. Some might say too friendly. Everyone liked her and she was always happy and pleasant."

Kelly's eyebrows rose. "That's not the impression Annie gave. She gave the impression she was reserved and wary of people."

"Annie would know best because she was closer with her," Ettie said.

"Then, why weren't the two of you close friends of hers?"

"No real reason," Ettie said. "Maybe because she lived on the other side of town. It makes visiting harder."

He eyed Ettie in the rear-view mirror. "Is there something the two of you are keeping from me?"

Elsa-May answered. "No. Not at all. We're telling you everything we know, but the thing is, there's nothing much to tell. She was a friendly woman who lived by herself, and she did give me a jigsaw puzzle a few weeks ago, so I guess you could say she was generous and kind as well. She was worried about me knitting so much. Mary must have told her that's what I do. One day she came to our place with a jigsaw puzzle for me—"

Kelly held up his hand. "Mrs. Smith told me about that briefly. Undoubtedly, it's a very interesting story. Why don't you tell me about it another time?"

"Okay. I will. I wasn't going to waste your time. I was trying to show you something of Deena's nature."

Kelly's eyes glazed over and he nodded. "Right. Who were her close friends besides Annie and Wayne Stoltzfus?" he asked.

Ettie recalled Annie saying that Deena had more admirers than just Wayne, but she took it that Kelly meant female friends. "The bishop's wife, Mary. Deena was friendly with everyone, but possibly no one in particular."

Detective Kelly said, “Hmm. It’s all a bit fuzzy if you ask me. You ladies weren’t friends with her and she gives you a gift of a puzzle, of all things, and then this woman has no friends, or does she?”

“If we knew more, we’d tell you,” Elsa-May said. “I think I need to apologize. I was wrong just now, Annie’s explanation of her is closer to the reality.”

Ettie opened her mouth and stared at Elsa-May. That was the first time she remembered Elsa-May admitting to being wrong.

“Annie was her friend and her sister-in-law. Nice to find that out when I did,” Kelly grumbled.

“That’s right.” Ettie looked out the window, wishing she had more to say. “Maybe you’ll find out more when you go to Deena’s house.”

“I certainly couldn’t find out any less than you two have told me.”

“Have you called Deena’s son?” Elsa-May asked.

“I left a message on his answering service. He hasn’t called back as yet.”

“We don’t even know where he lives, do we, Ettie?”

“No, we don’t. He could live anywhere.”

Kelly said, “Mrs. Smith, would you be kind enough to come into the station and make a statement tomorrow morning?”

“Okay, I’d be happy to, but there’s nothing I haven’t already told you.”

“Think about it overnight, there might be some small detail you’ve overlooked.”

"Did you find that white dog?" Ettie asked.

"No, but my men are canvassing the area looking for it and the victim's shoe, and anything else the dog might've removed from the scene." Kelly pulled up at their house. "Here we are. Home sweet home."

Ettie was glad to be home after their dreadful time. "Would you care to come in for a cup of hot tea, Detective Kelly?"

"He prefers coffee, Ettie."

"No thank you, Mrs. Smith. I'll keep moving. It's going to end up being another long day."

Elsa-May got out of the car. "We'll see you tomorrow morning."

Ettie and Elsa-May walked into their house and as soon as Ettie reached the living room, she collapsed onto the couch and put up her feet. Snowy spun around in circles showing he was pleased they were home.

"Poor Snowy. He didn't know we'd be gone this long." Elsa-May scooped him into her arms. "Just as well we left the dog door open for you." Elsa-May then put Snowy down on the floor, sat in her usual chair and picked up her knitting. "Back to normality."

Ettie was restless and knew for certain she wouldn't be able to sleep that night. Something they must do tomorrow was have a look through Deena's house. Looking up, she saw Elsa-May busy with her knitting, and smiling. She'd leave it until tomorrow to break the news about where they'd go.

CHAPTER 6

Ettie had been right. She wasn't able to sleep that night and was up early and made herself a cooked breakfast of sausages and eggs, so she'd have energy to see herself through the day.

Elsa-May woke just as Ettie was halfway through eating.

"Nice of you to wait." Elsa-May sat down at the kitchen table staring at her half-finished puzzle.

"Don't worry. I didn't disturb your pieces too much. I had to clear myself a portion of table to eat off."

"Good."

"I didn't know how long you'd be asleep. Would you have preferred me to wake you?"

"*Nee.* I needed as much sleep as I could get."

"When I finish this mouthful, I'll cook you something."

"*Denke.* I'll get myself a cup of *kaffe* while I wait. It'll be nice to have someone cook me breakfast for a change."

Ettie knew her sister was niggling her. They always took it in turns to make the breakfast. This time, Ettie wasn't going to take the bait. She was way too tired for an argument this early in the day, and besides that, she still hadn't told her sister she wanted to look through Deena's house today.

Once they'd eaten breakfast and had cleaned up, it was still early, so Elsa-May settled down to do some more of her puzzle. "Time to think about Deena's murder again I suppose. I know you won't rest until the murderer is found. I think best when my hands are busy."

Ettie folded her arms and tapped her foot on the ground. It would be much more comfortable sitting in the living room. "But how can you think about Deena when you're deciding which puzzle piece to put where?"

"Never interrupt someone doing a puzzle, Ettie. You might get a few cross words." Elsa-May chuckled.

"If that's a joke it makes no sense because it's not a crossword, it's a jigsaw puzzle. No!"

Elsa-May had just popped her glasses on and she looked over the top of them. "No puzzle?"

"No, to sitting here. Let's go into the living room because that's where I think best. There is something I want to discuss with you."

"What?" Elsa-May looked up.

Just as Ettie had her mouth open to speak, there was a knock at the door.

"That's a familiar knock," Elsa-May said.

"It's not loud enough to be Detective Kelly."

"Then go see who it is." Elsa-May made shooing motions with her hands.

Ettie opened their front door to their friend, the owner of the house next door, Gabriel.

"Come in." At that moment, Ettie guessed her plans for the day might change. "Elsa-May, it's Gabriel. Come out and say hello."

Elsa-May walked out of the kitchen, while Gabriel took off his hat. He nodded to the both of them and Ettie took his hat and put it on the peg by the door as he smoothed down his hair.

"Have you heard—?"

"About Deena Brown? *Jah,* it's terrible. Very sad. I heard she was murdered."

Elsa-May nodded. "That's what they say."

"I'm selling my house," he announced.

"Oh, the one next door?" Elsa-May blinked rapidly.

"*Jah,* that's the one. I'm not going to sell the one I'm living in. I only bought the one next to you because the price was so low."

"That's because it's a murder house," Elsa-May whispered.

"I know, but it didn't bother me, so it might not bother someone else. I thought it would've been a convenient place for visitors coming to our community. That hasn't worked out so far."

"Care for a hot cup of tea?" Ettie asked.

"I'd love one."

"Let's sit in the kitchen so we can get the last of the morning sun."

When they were all seated at the kitchen table with hot tea, Elsa-May said, "Sorry about the puzzle in the way. I daren't move it. I've been working on it for some time."

"It's fine."

"No one's stayed in your *haus* for a long time," Elsa-May said.

"That's why I'm selling it." He cleared his throat. "I'm here to ask a favor. I'm going away soon and I'm wondering if you and Ettie would be able to show people through it when I'm gone."

"Potential buyers?" Elsa-May asked.

"That's right."

Ettie frowned. "What about a realtor?"

"Nee. They charge fees. I'll hammer in a for sale sign and put a few notices around town. There should be some interest since I'm selling it for a low price. I'll give you a key." He reached into his pocket and pulled out a key. "You can show people through, *jah?"*

Ettie was taken aback. He assumed they'd do it and she didn't want to say no. It was too big of a responsibility, but it would give them the first chance to meet some possible new neighbors.

Elsa-May leaned forward and grabbed the key.

"What do we do if someone wants to buy it?" Ettie asked.

"Don't put the cart before the horse," Elsa-May said. "We haven't even shown it yet."

"I have a lawyer in town who will handle everything for me. I'll give you his details. He'll get in contact with me if there's anything I need to sign. I'm not expecting to sell it in a hurry."

Ettie studied his face. "Where are you going?"

"I'm visiting some relatives in Hazelton, Luzerne County, for the next few months. I won't be that far away."

Elsa-May got up and put the key into a jar on a top shelf in their small pantry. "Leave an address and a phone number for us, will you?"

"I'll do that before I leave."

"When are you going?" Ettie asked.

"I was going the day after tomorrow, but now I might wait around for Deena's funeral."

Ettie wasn't going to let an opportunity pass her by. "You're probably young enough to remember Ryker Lapp?"

"Oh yes, I remember him. I haven't seen him for years. I guess we'll see him at the funeral."

"What do you know about him?" Elsa-May asked.

"Last thing I heard was that he left us."

"That's correct."

"Are you asking because of what happened to Deena?"

"That's right. What can you tell us about him, or about Deena?"

"Do you mean that Deena wasn't his birth mother?"

"She wasn't?" Ettie and Elsa-May stared at each other.

"Only a few of us knew. He didn't get along with her. It upset him dreadfully when his father left. Stepfather, I guess he was, or was it his adopted father? Something like that. Either way, Ryker was never the same after that."

"In what way?"

"Never happy, and he was moody. He had stories about Deena." He chuckled. "He was an excellent storyteller."

"What made you think they were stories?" Elsa-May asked. "Deena was just a sweet woman."

"I'm not so sure about that," Ettie said under her breath.

The smile left his face. "What do you mean? Is there something going on that I should know?"

"Just a whole lot of talk that could be nonsense." Ettie picked up her teacup.

"What else do you remember about Ryker and the family?"

"About what?" he asked.

"Ryker," Elsa-May said.

"I can't think of anything. What kind of information are you looking for?"

"Anything, anything that seemed out of the ordinary to do with him and Deena."

He scratched the back of his neck. "Can't think of anything."

"What do you know about Hezekiah?" Ettie asked.

"He disappeared without a trace. That's all I remember of it. Why do you ask?" He looked from one to the other. "You're both scaring me right now."

"Well, it is a scary thing. Deena has been killed and we don't know who did it."

"It wasn't me," he said.

"No we know it wouldn't have been you, but when was the last time you saw her?"

"About a week ago. I drove past her. She was in trouble. The wheel of her buggy was caught in a ditch on the side of the road. I helped her out of it."

"On the side of the road?" Ettie asked. "Not on the road itself?"

"That's right."

Elsa-May frowned. "Where was she exactly?"

"Just on a stretch of road out toward the old deserted mill."

"I wonder what she was doing out that way." Ettie tapped a finger on her chin.

"She said she'd been sketching the mill."

Elsa-May said, "She was the creative type. Drawing

might have been a hobby of hers just as I enjoy knitting, puzzles, and the occasional crossword."

Ettie looked back at Gabriel. "So, that's the last time you saw her?"

"That sounds about right." Gabriel drained the last of his tea. "Now, I'm off to inform the lawyer that he might be getting a call from you two."

"I hope you get a high price for the *haus,*" Ettie told him.

"I just want it sold. If I get back what I paid for it, I'll be happy."

"We'll see what we can do," Elsa-May said staring at her puzzle. Then she picked up a piece and fitted it in a space. "There. Another one down."

Ettie shook her head. "I'll walk you out, Gabriel."

"Denke. I'll be back to see you before I go, but don't forget I'm not leaving just yet. Oh, and tell the potential buyers I can have the electrical wiring put back. That can be included in the price."

"That's right. The last two people who owned the house were *Englishers,* and the next ones could be, too. They'll be concerned about wiring."

After Ettie waved Gabriel off, she headed back to the kitchen and sat down with Elsa-May.

CHAPTER 7

"Gabriel said he might wait for the funeral, Ettie."

"Yes, I heard him. We have to get to the bottom of this. It's weird."

"It is. What makes it even more so is the note that was left at Annie's. And, how do you suggest we get to the bottom of it? We don't even know how she died yet."

"We know enough. We know Deena was murdered and we know someone tried to make everyone think she was still alive, and of course, that had to have been the murderer." Ettie tapped on her chin. "I wonder if someone is hiding in Deena's house and that's why they wanted to make it look like she was still alive—so they'd not go near the house."

"They would've got a fright when Kelly went there,

and the forensic team before him." A chuckle tumbled from Elsa-May's lips.

"Annie said she thought she heard noises in the house the day she went there, but Deena would've already been dead."

"Where does this go?" Elsa-May looked down at the puzzle, searching where to place the piece she held in her hand.

Ettie tried to bring the conversation back to Deena's house so that Elsa-May would come to the conclusion they had to go through it. "Me too. I'd reckon the clue lies somewhere in her house."

"Why would you think that? It doesn't seem like she was killed there," Elsa-May said.

"Kelly should learn that today. His experts can tell if Deena had been moved after she died."

"I suppose they can."

Ettie knew it was useless, she'd just have to come out with it. "This is what we'll do, we'll go to her house and see what we can find."

Elsa-May shook her head. "Not me. Kelly said to stay out of his way. I'm not going to risk seeing his angry face."

"You said you'd help and now you're not willing?"

Elsa-May fitted another piece in one corner. "I said I'd help you think. Going through a dead person's house, uninvited, is not thinking. It's the opposite of thinking, it's doing."

Snowy walked into the room and looked at them.

"He's wondering why we're in here and not in the living room. You'd come with me to Deena's *haus,* wouldn't you, Snowy, if you were a person?" Ettie smiled at Snowy, the way he stopped still and looked into her face. "He says, yes, he would."

Elsa-May giggled. "You're talking with animals now?"

"They make more sense than people sometimes."

"Annie seems to think so. Her cats are her *kinner.*"

Ettie tapped on her chin. "I wonder if the police will ever find that white dog."

"*Nee,* Ettie, they haven't found him yet. We asked him that." Elsa-May picked up another puzzle piece.

"I said I wonder if they ever will. I know they haven't found him yet."

"Before you suggest it, I'm going to say I'm not going out on the streets knocking on doors looking for that dog. Does the dog really exist outside your imagination, Ettie?"

"I saw it as plain as day."

"In your mind's eye, or for real?"

"For real, and he took a shoe. One of Deena's shoes is missing, so that should be proof enough for you that the dog is real. I didn't imagine it. The police wouldn't look for a dog unless they knew it was missing."

"What, the dog or the shoe?" Elsa-May chuckled.

"Both! I don't know why you doubt me so much."

Elsa-May sighed. "Habits are hard to break."

"It's not nice to think the worst of me all the time."

Ettie pouted.

"That's nonsense. I don't think the worst of you at all. I'm joking most of the time, just having a little fun. Do you want to know what I really think of you?"

Ettie smiled and nodded. All she wanted from her older sister was a kind word or two of appreciation.

"I think you're good," Elsa-May stated.

There it was. Ettie was delighted to finally hear something positive. "You really think so?"

"That's right you're good—good for nothing." Elsa-May threw her head back and cackled.

Ettie was disgusted with her sister and her mean words. She'd had enough. Ettie grabbed the edge of the table and pulled herself to her feet. "C'mon, Snowy. I'm taking you for a walk."

"It's all right, I can do that later."

"*Nee.* You can take him on another walk if you want."

"Suit yourself. You usually do."

Ettie walked to the front door and grabbed the leash from off the peg. Snowy followed her and sat at her feet. She leaned down and clipped the leash onto his collar before she called out to Elsa-May, "I can't say how long we'll be gone."

Elsa-May hollered back, "No hurry. Take your time. Enjoy the scenery on this beautiful morning. Enjoy spying on the neighbors as you pass by their houses, and please don't find any more bodies."

Ettie closed the front door behind her and walked

down the two porch steps mumbling about how rude Elsa-May was. Didn't she know words were hurtful?

Ettie walked Snowy fifteen minutes down the road trying to calm herself and wondering if she should move to a place of her own rather than share a home with her sister. When she was just about to head back to give Elsa-May a piece of her mind, she saw a buggy. She stopped and waited for it to get closer so she could see who it was.

The buggy pulled up alongside her. It was Maggie Overberg, one of the ladies who would've been at Annie's quilting bee yesterday.

"Ettie, have you heard?"

Ettie walked closer. *"Jah,* I have, sadly. Elsa-May and I were there yesterday when Deena was found. It was awful, so sad." Ettie was careful not to tell Maggie too much. The woman was a dreadful gossip.

"Everyone knows that. I'm not talking about that."

Ettie stared at her wondering what else could've happened. "What is it?"

"The police have Annie Lapp in jail for killing Deena Brown."

"What?" Ettie shrieked.

"Jah, Ettie. The police have taken Annie, for killing Deena."

Had Ettie heard right?

Their old friend Annie?

What could've happened? They saw her just yesterday.

CHAPTER 8

"No! That's not possible. We were just with Annie yesterday morning and..." If what Maggie said was correct, why hadn't Detective Kelly told them he had arrested their friend?

"It happened last night. It's true. I'm not making up stories."

"I wouldn't think you were making it up, Maggie. I know you're not." Ettie found it hard to take in. "There must be some mistake."

"Annie asked the bishop to tell you and he wanted to stay at the police station where she's locked up, so he talked to Mary, who sent me to tell you."

Ettie's fingertips flew to her mouth. It had to be true. Annie had been arrested. "*Denke* for letting me know. I'll have to tell Elsa-May."

"I'll drive you home."

"It's okay. I can walk that far." She glanced over her shoulder at her house. "It's not far," Ettie repeated.

"Are you all right, Ettie?"

"I will be when this sinks in. I can't think why they arrested her."

"They think she killed her, that's why. I'll keep moving, Ettie. I have others who need to know." She jiggled the reins and then the horse and buggy moved away.

"Denke, Maggie," Ettie called after her.

"I'll see you on Sunday if not before," Maggie yelled back with her head halfway out the buggy's window.

Ettie stood still, in total shock. Why would the police think for a moment that old Annie killed Deena?

There was one way to find out.

She had to call Kelly.

Ettie hurried to the shanty that housed the telephone. When Ettie reached it, she realized she had no coins to put in the honesty tin. She'd do that later. Ettie grabbed the phone's receiver and dialed Detective Kelly's number that she knew by heart.

After six ring tones, it went to message. She tried again, and after it went to message a second time, she hung up.

"Let's go home, Snowy. We'll see what Elsa-May thinks of this."

Several minutes later, Elsa-May sat stunned on hearing the news. One of her puzzle pieces had fallen to the floor and she stared at Ettie, unconcerned about it. "We only just left her yesterday and Detective Kelly didn't even suspect her! He's the one leading the investigation."

"I know! I heard it from Maggie Overberg. I tried to call Kelly, but there was no answer."

"Did you call the police station?"

"I only had his cell phone number in my head. I don't know the number of the police station. What should we do?"

"We'll go to Annie's house to see that Smokie and Blacky are looked after."

"That's Pepper and Smokie, Elsa-May."

"That's what I said."

"You said Blacky and Smokie."

"What does it matter, Ettie? Who cares what they're called? I'm surprised you even remember."

"It matters to Annie. Poor Annie sitting in a jail cell with no food or water. And no sewing and no comfortable chairs, worried about her cats. All the while, accused of murdering her friend, who's possibly her best friend in the world."

Elsa-May leaned down to retrieve the fallen piece. "If you'll remember, she said that she wasn't a friend. Annie was trying to be a friend to her, but it was obvious that Deena wasn't reciprocating."

Ettie couldn't believe how Elsa-May was nit-picking the facts while their friend was sitting in a jail cell. "We'll feed the cats and then there's the horse. Has he been fed?"

"We saw two horses, remember?"

"Ah yes."

"Well, surely the bishop will have someone see to the livestock," Elsa-May said.

"*Jah,* but we don't know for certain, and those poor kitties. The horses won't starve, they'll have grass at least if they don't get fed and I saw yesterday that they had a full water trough. They have enough water for a week even if it doesn't rain. The kitties will run out of food and water fairly soon."

"Let's go."

Ettie stood up.

Elsa-May frowned as she held the puzzle piece in her hand. "Just as soon as I find where this piece fits. Otherwise, it'll bug me all day."

Ettie sat down again. It didn't look like Elsa-May had made progress with the puzzle all day. "When I woke up yesterday morning, I had no idea all this would've happened in a few small hours. How quickly lives can change."

Elsa-May sighed. "I know what you mean. Ah, there it is." Elsa-May tried to fit the piece into the space.

"It's not the right place."

Elsa-May looked up. "I know that. It looked like it would fit, though, until I tried it."

Ettie grimaced. The puzzle would be cluttering up their kitchen table for months if her sister only placed two or three pieces a day. "Try there." Ettie pointed to a spot not far from the one Elsa-May had just tried.

Elsa-May slotted it in and then grinned. "Perfect."

"Great, let's get moving."

"Yes, poor Smokie and Stormy must be starving by now."

Ettie opened her mouth to correct her sister's error, but she decided, this one time, to ignore it.

CHAPTER 9

It was mid-morning by the time a taxi brought Ettie and Elsa-May to Annie's house. Yellow crime scene tape wrapped around the trees that enclosed the area where Deena had been found.

They walked up the driveway.

"What reason would they have for thinking she killed Deena? There must be some mistake," Elsa-May said.

"We'll have to find out from Kelly as soon as we can. Let's just make certain her beloved cats are okay first before I call him again."

"I know we're going to feed the kitties. That's why we're here. You're saying something that's obvious again. Stating the obvious."

Ettie didn't say anything. She knew Elsa-May was upset and if she responded, they'd both get more bothered than they were already. When they stood at the front door, Ettie said, “You go in first.”

Elsa-May moved forward, put her hand on the door handle and turned it both ways. “It’s locked.”

“I can hear meowing. They must be hungry. Poor kitties.” Ettie took a turn at trying the door handle.

“Step back.” Elsa-May elbowed Ettie in the stomach, causing Ettie to move. Elsa-May then bent down and lifted the mat. Underneath it was a key.

“How did you know that was there?” Ettie asked, as Elsa-May held it up.

“I didn’t.” Elsa-May fitted the key in the lock and turned it to the right. A loud click sounded. “We’re in.” Elsa-May pushed the door open.

“Don’t let the cats out.”

As soon as they were both inside and the door was shut behind them, the cats were there, pawing at them and meowing.

“Let’s see what we can find you to eat. *Mamm* will be home soon, I know she will be.”

“Ettie, don’t bother, they can’t understand what you’re saying.”

“I think they can. Look at how they ran to the kitchen as soon as I said eat.”

“You look after the kitties, I’ll check on the horse.”

“Horses,” Ettie corrected, “and don’t do that alone. I’ll come with you after I’m done here. Help me find the cat food.”

The cats were now at their food bowls, still meowing. Elsa-May opened a cupboard and lifted out a large container and then removed the lid. "This looks like kibble."

"Let me see." Ettie had a sniff. "Smells fishy. Give that to them while I fill their water bowls, then you can change their kitty litter."

Elsa-May pointed to herself. "Me?"

"That's right."

While Ettie filled the bowls with water from the sink, she thought of all the reasons Kelly might have arrested Annie. Nothing came to mind. Ettie put the water bowls back down for the cats. "The police must have evidence, Elsa-May. They can't arrest someone for nothing. So, what evidence would they have?"

"A witness?"

"Who?"

"Someone we don't know about. What about Wayne?"

"It's possible," Ettie said. "He might have told Kelly something. That makes sense in one way but not in another."

"What do you mean?"

"It makes sense timing-wise because Kelly went to Wayne's house last night, but it doesn't make sense in another way because we know Annie is innocent."

Elsa-May dusted off her hands. "Innocent Annie."

"Well, don't you think so?"

"*Jah,* I do."

"Then why say innocent Annie like that?"

"Because I agree with you. I think she's innocent. When Detective Kelly left here, he was heading to Deena's place. If Wayne didn't say anything about Annie, then the detective must've found something in Deena's house that pointed to Annie as the killer. I knew there was a clue at Deena's house, I said so."

Ettie held her tongue. She was the one who had said there had to be a clue in Deena's house. Nevertheless, she played along. It required less energy than arguing. "You might have been right."

"Why don't you clean the cat trays?" Elsa-May grumbled.

"Haven't you done that yet?"

"No!"

Ettie shook her head. "I've done my bit, you do yours. I'm too upset, and I'll do them next time. I'll look around here and see what I can find."

Elsa-May pressed her thin lips together, and then grumbled, "This is the worst job. The very worst. I'm glad I have a dog. There are two trays, so why don't we do one each? That makes it fair."

"No. If you're doing one, you might as well do the other. No sense us both having to scrub our hands afterward." Ettie left a complaining Elsa-May and headed to the living room. The first thing she noticed were the bags of fabric in the corner. She started sifting through them and stopped when there was nothing interesting to find, and besides that, she wasn't quite sure what she was looking for. Sinking into the couch, she thought some more.

If only she'd had more to do with Deena, and had been friendlier.

Ettie spied a piece of paper on the low table in front of the couch. It looked like it had been torn from a book. She leaned forward and grabbed the page. It was a plan for the quilt they were going to make. On the page was a list of which lady was coming to the quilting bee, along with which part of the quilt they were to work on.

Then Ettie narrowed her eyes as she noticed something interesting.

CHAPTER 10

The writing on the paper Ettie had found in Annie's house was small with long tails on the Gs and the Ys. Not dissimilar to the note supposedly left by Deena on the very morning her body was found.

Ettie clutched the paper tightly in her hand and headed out to the laundry room where Elsa-May was bending over changing the cat litter, and she was still complaining.

"Did you see the note that came from Deena?"

Elsa-May stood up. "Is this a trick question? We all know that Deena didn't write that note because she was already dead."

"Look at this." Ettie held the page out to Elsa-May. "I'm thinking that Annie herself was the author."

"Annie wrote a note to herself?"

"Annie wrote it pretending it was from Deena. I

found this, and it's Annie's handwriting. It looks so much like the writing on the paper that Detective Kelly took with him. If only we had it here, we could've compared the two side by side."

Elsa-May made a face. "Why would Annie do that?"

"I don't know yet, but I will find out." Ettie lowered the note down by her side. "I might be wrong, but it looks similar. Did you see the note before Kelly took it?"

"No."

"I did."

Elsa-May pushed out her lips, disapprovingly. "Just put that back where you found it. We don't want to make things worse for Annie."

"She's been arrested for murder. How much worse can things get?"

At that moment, they both heard a horse and buggy outside the house.

"You finish off what you're doing, and I'll see who it is." Ettie hurried out the front door. It was the bishop's wife, Mary, stepping down from her buggy.

Mary looked up and stopped still, when she saw Ettie. "You got my message from Maggie?"

"Yes. We're feeding the cats. Elsa-May's changing the litter trays."

"Denke, Ettie, that is very kind of both of you. Will you continue doing that until she gets home?"

"So it is true?"

Mary nodded. "I'm sad to say it is."

"I know, and when we came here and Annie wasn't home, I half believed it, but I couldn't quite believe it."

"No one can."

"What do you know about what's happened?" Ettie asked as she walked over to her.

Mary looped the reins over the hitching post and then leaned against it. "All I know is that she called Paul from the police station late last night. She said she was arrested for Deena's murder, but that's all I know. Paul went to the station hoping to get some answers and he still hasn't come home. We're praying he can bring Annie home with him today." Mary sighed. "And we haven't been able to get in touch with Luke."

"There's a mistake, obviously. Annie would never do anything like that."

"I know. Who would've killed Deena, though?" Mary lowered her head.

Ettie breathed in sharply. "I don't know. I wish I did. What do you know about Deena, Mary? Out of anyone, you would've known her best."

Mary gave a slight shrug. "She joined us when Ryker was a baby. After a few months with us, she married Hezekiah Lapp. Annie's brother-in-law."

"And what was the marriage like?" Ettie asked, knowing that the bishop's wife would know a great deal more about personal lives than someone else might.

"Hezekiah was much older, and he was a widower, as you know. He had no *kinner* of his own, so he was delighted Deena had a son. For that reason alone it was a convenient pairing. *Gott* found two people who needed what the other had to offer and he brought them together."

"So they got along?" Ettie asked.

"They did."

"I remember their wedding, but only vaguely." Ettie wondered if Mary knew Ryker wasn't Deena's son. Surely she would've, but why hadn't she mentioned that? If Gabriel knew it, then Mary had to know it.

"I'm not surprised you don't remember it well, Ettie. It was more than twenty years ago."

"Do you know anything about her life before she joined us?" Ettie asked.

"No. The past is the past, and in Deena's case, I think she wanted it behind her."

"Why do you say that?"

When Mary's eyes flickered around the place, Ettie knew there was more to Deena's story. She had to find out. "Was she in some kind of trouble when she arrived here?"

"No. I don't think so, but I'm often not told things. People like to keep things to themselves, especially dark secrets."

"Secrets? Deena had secrets? Do you think one of those secrets might have gotten her killed?"

"Oh, I've said too much. Ettie, you do have a way with you. I hadn't meant to say as much as I have."

Elsa-May approached them wiping her hands on a

small towel. "Mary, it's lovely to see you. Do you have news of Annie?"

"Nee. I was just telling Ettie that Paul is waiting at the police station to see what he can find out. He's hoping to bring Annie home."

"That's not likely if she's been arrested. She'll have to wait to go before a judge tomorrow morning. I think that's how it works."

Ettie frowned at Elsa-May. "We don't know that for a fact. I'm certain the detective has the choice to let her go, and he will as soon as he realizes his error."

"If you say so, Ettie." Then Elsa-May looked at Mary. "What about Deena? Is there any further news on her and how she might've died?"

Mary took a step away from the hitching post. "You two with your questions. I don't know the answers to any of them. If you visit us tomorrow, Paul might know something." Mary fixed a smile on her face and then stepped past them. *"Denke,* for seeing to the cats for Annie. She will be pleased someone's taking care of them. I should go. I've got so many things to get done."

Ettie unlooped the reins and handed them to her.

"All the women in the community are dreadfully worried."

"All of them?" Ettie wondered how she could possibly know that.

"Well, all the ladies from the quilting team. They're worried about a murderer on the loose and they want to come up with a plan to keep themselves safe." Mary climbed up into the buggy and never said another word.

The sisters watched Mary turn her horse and buggy around and head back toward the road.

"She said something about Deena having secrets. I wonder what she meant." Ettie bit her lip. "Possibly, she doesn't want to tell us Deena's secret about Ryker not being her birthchild."

"Why didn't you ask her?"

"I don't know. I was waiting for her to say it."

"Ettie, we need to..." Elsa-May hesitated.

"What is it?" Ettie asked.

"It was something we had to do today. Now, I completely forget what it was."

"I think you were going to say that we must find out what Deena's secrets were."

"No! That's obvious. It wasn't that. Whatever it is, it'll come back to me. But we also need to find out why Annie was arrested and why Detective Kelly didn't let us know."

"I know. That is odd. He normally keeps us informed about things to do with our community."

Elsa-May tucked the small hand towel under her arm. "He told us to keep out of his way, but didn't he also ask us to find out what we could?"

"He probably didn't mean it. That was his way of keeping a couple of silly old fools out of his hair."

"What silly old fools. Oh, you mean us?"

"That's right."

"I see."

Ettie looked over to where the body had been found. "Deena was found on Annie's property." Ettie walked over and stopped at the perimeter of the crime scene tape.

Elsa-May followed and stood beside her. "Why here?"

"That's what Kelly asked himself. Why here?" Ettie faced her sister. "What if he found out that Annie wrote that note and that's why he arrested her? That would make sense, and it would be the only thing that makes sense. Why would she have done it? It's so odd."

"How long does it take for fingerprints to be verified?" Elsa-May asked.

"They can do that fairly quickly. Maybe they thought she wrote the note because it matched her handwriting and possibly hers were the only fingerprints on the note. If she wrote it, that meant she wanted everyone to think Deena was still alive and they wouldn't look for her body. That might be enough to arrest her."

"*Jah,* but everyone would've figured Deena was missing when she never showed at the meetings," Ettie said. "As far as we know, Annie never had a reason to kill Deena. Besides that, she would never do that to anyone. At least, the Annie we thought we knew wouldn't." Ettie looked back to the raked-up dirt where

Deena had been found. "I think it's time we had a look through Deena's house."

"No! I'm not going. It's getting dark."

Ettie stared at Elsa-May. "It's not even midday yet."

"A woman's been murdered, Ettie, and we both know that Annie didn't do it. That means the murderer is out there somewhere. Possibly hiding inside Deena's home."

"Whoever was hiding would've gotten a fright when Kelly arrived." Ettie smiled.

"Well, he was probably gone by then, but he could've been hiding there."

"Maybe."

"Annie said she heard noises in Deena's home. Why don't we go home? First thing tomorrow, we'll talk with Bishop Paul and Detective Kelly. This could be solved by then and Annie might be free."

Ettie looked back at the dug-up earth that had been Deena's resting place. If it weren't for Elsa-May, she would've gone to Deena's home right now, but she had to consider Elsa-May. Her sister wasn't getting any younger. "Okay. We'll do as you say."

"I'll call us a taxi."

CHAPTER 11

"What do we know about Ryker?" Ettie asked, as they walked to the barn where the phone was kept.

"He left years ago. That's all I know."

"Only around ten years ago or so when he was a young teen. I can't tell you when it was, the years get away from me."

"What do I remember about him? Let's see. Nothing really. I don't think I ever spoke to him." Elsa-May shook her head.

"Wasn't he around the same age as Peter, Joshua's son—your grandson?"

"It's a possibility."

"Perhaps we should talk with Peter," Ettie suggested.

"What, today?"

"*Jah,* we can stop by his place on the way home."

Doing something—anything was better than going home and watching Elsa-May do her puzzle at the rate of one piece every two hours. The way she was going, she might still be doing it in another ten years.

"Will that help anything?" Elsa-May asked. "I would do it if I thought it would help Annie get out of jail."

"It might. Who better to know a mother's secrets than her son? Maybe Ryker talked to his friends."

"You think Deena had secrets?" Elsa-May asked.

"I know it. That's what slipped out of Mary's mouth."

Elsa-May sighed. "It won't hurt to see if he knows anything about Ryker and what he's been doing. But first, we should visit Wayne."

Ettie was delighted at the prospect of going somewhere else as well. They called a taxi to take them to Wayne's house.

"I hope he's home after this," Elsa-May said as they walked up the short driveway to Wayne's small house.

"I've got a feeling he will be."

When they reached the front door, they saw it was slightly ajar. Ettie moved it a little and then called out, "Hello, hello? Are you there, Wayne?"

The door slowly opened wider and a figure stood in front of them. Because she'd been in the bright sun, Ettie couldn't focus very well. "Is that you, Wayne?"

"It is, Ettie. Come inside. Hello, Elsa-May. I didn't see you standing there."

"Hello, Wayne." They stepped into the house.

"We're so sorry to hear about Deena," Elsa-May said.

He nodded.

"Could I trouble you for a glass of water?" Ettie asked. "We've just come from Annie's."

"Come into the kitchen."

Once they were seated with glasses of water, Ettie began, "Did a detective come and ask you some questions last night or yesterday?"

"He did. I can't remember what he said. I was too much in shock after Bishop Paul told me the dreadful news."

"Yes, well that is understandable."

"Would you like something else to drink? I have lemonade."

"No, we're fine with water, but thanks, Wayne. I'll come straight to the point. Do you know anyone who wanted to harm Deena?"

"Why, did someone say I wanted to?"

Elsa-May and Ettie exchanged glances.

"No, we haven't heard anything like that at all. Why would you say that?"

"People laughed behind my back."

"About what?" Ettie asked.

"I paid her to help me feed my livestock every day and it was nice to have her companionship."

"Why would anybody find anything funny about that?" asked Elsa-May.

"Because when I took her back to her place, I helped her with hers—unpaid, of course."

"But she's only got one horse, hasn't she?"

"That's right. I would help her feed him and exercise him if she hadn't taken him out for a few days, and that kind of thing."

"Take the horse to the blacksmith?" Elsa-May suggested.

"Yes, that too. I would pay her to work and then I'd work at her place for nothing."

"I see, that makes sense," Elsa-May said.

"Do you think that's worth laughing at, Elsa-May?"

"I don't, but I can see why some people would."

Ettie wanted to get to the point. "So do you know if Deena had any enemies or anybody who would have wanted to do her harm?"

He grunted. "The detective was asking the same thing. I can't think of one single person who would want to hurt her. She was such a sweet and mellow-tempered woman." His eyes misted over.

"Yes, she was," Elsa-May said.

"It's a funny thing. Hezekiah went missing and now she's dead."

"Why's that funny?" Ettie asked.

"Things like that don't happen around here, and it's happened in the one family. I must say that Luke, Hezekiah's brother, was never the same after he disappeared."

Ettie scratched her neck. Luke was due back soon,

Annie had said.

"Is that so?" Elsa-May asked.

"In what way?" Ettie moved forward in her seat.

"In every way. I suppose Mr. Thripp from the store in town has heard about her death. He'll be upset."

"Mr. Thripp?" Ettie asked.

"I've heard of him," Elsa-May said. "He owns Amish Dinner."

Then their attention was taken by a white dog walking into the room. Ettie recognized it immediately and nudged Elsa-May in the ribs.

Wayne smiled. "Snowy, where have you been?"

Elsa-May said, "We have a dog called Snowy, too, but he's much smaller than yours."

"Do you?" He patted his dog.

"We do."

Ettie wondered, should she tell him that his dog ran off with Deena's shoe, or just tell Detective Kelly? She looked at Elsa-May hoping she'd get a nod, or a shake of her head that would tell her what to do. When she saw Elsa-May frown, she decided to keep quiet.

"How long have you had the dog?" Elsa-May asked.

"About five years now."

"And you just let him roam about the place?"

He looked across at Elsa-May. "Can't keep him in. Won't you have a glass of lemonade?"

"No thank you." Ettie stood up. "We should go."

"Already?" Elsa-May stared up at her.

"Wayne, I have to tell you something." Ettie sat

back down.

"What is it?" Wayne asked.

"This is awful, and it's uncomfortable for me to even say it."

He gulped. "Go on."

"I was the one who found her."

Wayne nodded. "I know. I heard that and it must've been awful."

"It was and… I saw your dog digging close to where Deena lay. I clapped my hands to scare him off and then he ran away with Deena's shoe."

Wayne scratched the side of his face. "Ran off with a shoe?"

"*Jah,* and I had no idea he was your dog, but it was. He's quite distinctive looking. There wouldn't be another dog around that looks like him."

"I haven't seen a shoe about the place."

Elsa-May took a large gulp of water and then set the glass down. "Does he bring things home with him? I once had a dog named Ginger, and he used to bring odd things home. He was like one of those wood rats they call a pack rat."

Wayne shook his head. "No, he doesn't bring things to the house. But, I can have a look around."

"Didn't Detective Kelly see the dog when he was here?"

Elsa-May added, "He was sending the officers up and down the farms on this stretch of road to look for the dog."

"He didn't mention anything. I don't know where Snowy was at the time, but no one ever asked me about a dog."

Ettie asked, "Do you mind if we tell the detective we've found the dog?"

"He'll need the shoe for evidence," Elsa-May told him.

"Wait a minute." He got up and walked to the kitchen drawers and opened one. Then he came back and sat down with a card in his hand. "This is what the detective gave me. It's got his phone number there on the bottom."

"Would you like me to call him?" Ettie asked.

"I can do it."

"Denke."

"He'll be happy we've located him." Elsa-May smiled.

"I hope Snowy's not in trouble," Wayne said.

"Nee, of course not. They just want to locate the shoe and see if there was anything else Snowy might have taken from the scene."

Wayne nodded. "I'll call him soon. Can I take you ladies home?"

"We're not going straight home, but would you be kind enough to call us a taxi?"

"I can do that."

"We'll wait down by the road."

As they walked out of the house, Ettie whispered, "I hope I've done the right thing. What if he finds it and picks it up?"

"The shoe?"

"Yes."

"I don't think he'll find anything. He probably won't even look. He seemed too upset to look for his dead girlfriend's shoe."

"You're right. It would be awful. He's calling Detective Kelly, so we've done our bit."

"It's funny that his dog has the same name as mine."

"Not really. What else would someone call a white dog?"

"Oh, Ettie, they could call it anything."

Ettie shrugged. "I know, but it's white, get it? How do you think Ginger got his name?"

Elsa-May frowned. "You don't just name a dog by its color, you know. There are a host of other names that would fit a white dog, even if you did name the dog by the color. There's Blizzard, Whitey, Ghost, Snowflake, and many others I can think of."

"That's right. You're right." Ettie sighed.

"I know I am." They looked up to see a taxi already heading toward them. "That was fast. Also, what about Pepper and Blackie, you can't tell me that Annie..."

Ettie didn't bother correcting Elsa-May about the cats' names and zoned out as her sister kept talking about animals and how they might have gotten their names.

CHAPTER 12

A short time later, they were on property that belonged to one of Elsa-May's grandsons—who was, of course, also Ettie's grandnephew. He had a small house on the edge of his father's farm where they raised whatever crops were most in demand.

They got out of the taxi and sent it away. As they walked up the driveway, Ettie said, "I've got a hunch."

"I hope you brought enough for two. I'm hungry."

Ettie frowned at her sister. "I said a *hunch,* not lunch."

"Oh. Well, let's hear it."

"We should go to the Amish Dinner."

"For lunch?" Elsa-May asked.

"Forget about food, will you?"

"You're the one who keeps talking about it and it's not a diner and they don't serve meals. Amish Dinner is a small goods store."

"Nee, I don't want anything to eat. I want to go there to find out about Mr. Thripp, the owner. He was supposed to be a friend of Deena's. Didn't you hear what Wayne said?"

"Okay. We can do that tomorrow. It's getting a bit late today and—"

Ettie was disappointed. "I know, your feet are sore."

"How did you remember?" Elsa-May asked.

Ettie let out a long drawn out sigh.

Peter appeared, framed by a window at the front of the house, waved, and then came out to meet them. *"Mammi,* and Aunt Ettie. What are you two doing here? You never visit."

"We are today. We've come to check up on you." Elsa-May reached up and patted his shoulder.

He laughed. "Check on me?"

"Jah."

"Nee, I'm not married yet if that's what you've come to ask, but I do have my eye on a young woman who could change my life for the better."

"We do have something to ask, but that wasn't one of the questions." Ettie looked back at the waiting taxi. The cents were ticking by. "We can't stay because we have a taxi waiting. Have you heard about Deena Brown?"

"I did."

"And about Annie Lapp?"

He nodded. "Maggie Overberg told us. She was at

the bishop's house and heard about it. Is that what you wanted to ask me?"

"What do you know about Ryker, Deena's son?"

He rubbed the back of his neck and then tipped his hat back on his head. "We were close friends before he left. Funny thing was, I thought I caught a glimpse of him in town recently. When I turned to look again, he was gone."

"What was their background before Deena joined the community?"

"All I remember is that Hezekiah was his stepfather. Ryker said his mother joined us when he was a baby and he was a little annoyed and said he never had a choice about joining the community. He always said he was going to leave and find out where he came from and learn who his 'real' family was."

"So you know Deena wasn't his birthmother?"

"*Jah,* all his friends knew. He often told us the story of how Deena snatched him from someone. She said that she told him the truth in a rage when he was… I don't know, he would've been about twelve or thirteen. I recall him telling me the day after he found out. That was what fired him up to find his family."

Ettie and Elsa-May looked at one another. "But he got along with both his parents even if they weren't his birthparents, didn't he?"

"Ettie, didn't you hear what he just said?" Elsa-May shook her head.

"I did, but I thought it might be a mistake."

Peter grimaced. "*Nee!* He didn't like Deena. He never said why, but he said the only adult he trusted was Hezekiah."

"Oh dear, and then Hezekiah left," Ettie said. "The poor boy. I feel sorry for him. It must've broken his heart when that happened."

"So, he was never close with Deena?" Elsa-May asked.

"That's the truth. The truth of what he said to me, anyway."

"What is the reason for that?" Ettie asked. "Did she beat him, was she mean to him? Did she send him to bed without any food?"

He sighed. "I don't like to repeat it because it sounds awful."

"You must tell us," Elsa-May demanded. Gone was her sweet grandmotherly tone.

"He said something along the lines of, she was hateful, and a spiteful person with a cold heart."

Ettie pictured Deena. "That's hard to believe. She's such a small woman and never looked that way at all."

"I'm just saying what he told me. She was mean to him and she was mean to her own husband. Didn't cook for him. She cooked for herself and Hezekiah had to cook separately for himself and Ryker. I didn't believe it, I thought he was making up stories, and then one day I was at his home and he showed me how she kept her food separate from theirs."

"That is odd."

"I saw it with my own eyes. Once he'd shown me the container of food with the label 'Deena! Don't touch!' I believed what he told me."

All at once, Ettie gasped and looked at Elsa-May. "Ach! I was supposed to make a statement today. I told Kelly I would."

"That's what I remembered earlier today."

"That was the thing you remembered and then forgot?" Ettie asked.

"It was."

Ettie sighed. "This isn't how I wanted things. We'll have to go there right now, and hope he isn't too angry with us."

"I hope we get some of our questions answered about why Annie's been arrested."

"I certainly hope so, too."

"Maybe Detective Kelly won't ever find out you forgot, Ettie. He said to come today to make a statement and it's still today."

Ettie smiled, feeling better. *"Jah,* you're right. It is still today."

"I can take you there," Peter offered. "Are you going to the police station in town?"

"That's the one," Elsa-May said, with a sigh. "but, I am rather tired. Oh dear."

Ettie didn't want to wear her sister out—neither of them was getting any younger. "Why don't we go home, and I'll make that statement first thing in the morning?"

Elsa-May nodded. "If you don't mind, Ettie. *Denke.*"

"I'll take you home, then," Peter said.

"We'd love that if it's not too much trouble." Elsa-May smiled sweetly.

"My horse could use the exercise. I haven't been doing much lately with my bad leg." He slapped his thigh.

"What's wrong with it?"

"A horse kicked me. It's okay. I don't think anything's broken. It's just a sprain or a bruise."

"You should get it checked out," Ettie told him.

"Nee denke. I'd rather put up with the pain. It'll come right eventually."

"Stubborn, just like your *grossmammi.*" Ettie laughed.

With a twinkle in his eye, Peter looked at his grandmother. "They do say that's where I get it from."

"Do they?" Elsa-May's mouth turned down at the corners, while Ettie laughed some more.

That night at home, Ettie was restless. As she tried to sleep, she kept imagining the look on the detective's face. He'd told her to come and make a statement and she said she would. She wasn't going to be just a little late, she was going to be a whole day late. Then an image of his disappointed face kept her awake the rest of the night.

CHAPTER 13

Early the next morning, Ettie and Elsa-May sat at the police station across the desk from Detective Kelly.

"Morning, ladies. I can finally say I got a call from a man about a dog."

"Wayne called you?" Elsa-May asked.

"Yes."

Elsa-May leaned forward. "You might want to have a chat with your deputies. Wayne said the police were there and they didn't ask if he had a dog."

Kelly shook his head. "It was I who was there, but I'm afraid I had other things on my mind at that time. The officers had spread out. I thought they would've reached his home to make their inquiries before I got there. When I arrived, your bishop was just leaving. Does that answer your query, Mrs. Lutz?"

"I didn't have a question."

"He said query, Elsa-May."

"Same difference."

Kelly raised his eyebrows. "Right now, I've got my men searching Wayne's property for the victim's missing shoe and anything else they might come across."

"I hope they find it. Now, Detective Kelly, might I ask if Annie Lapp is still here?"

"She is."

Elsa-May leaned across the desk. "I thought you'd let her out having found you made a mistake."

Detective Kelly glared at Elsa-May for that last comment. "Why did I arrest her?" He stared from one to the other. "I'll tell you in a moment. Mrs. Smith, you agreed to come here to make a statement yesterday morning. You show up twenty-four hours later than we agreed." He raised his hands in the air, palm-side up, waiting for an answer.

Ettie gulped. She opened her mouth to speak and then hesitated.

He lowered his arms and placed his palms down on the desk. "Did you forget?"

Elsa-May got impatient and spoke for her, "Yes, she forgot. Completely forgot, but she's here now."

Ettie's mouth fell open and she stared at her sister. "That's not the full truth. We did forget and then we remembered. One of us was feeling tired so the other had to go home with her." If it weren't for her sister, Ettie would only have been half a day late.

"I see. It does seem odd that you two go everywhere together, but each to their own. I do have some news. We arrived at Deena Brown's house to find it ransacked. Someone was looking for something. Perhaps it was Annie looking for any incriminating evidence against herself."

Elsa-May said, "Will you tell us why she's been arrested?"

"I never said she was arrested. She isn't, but I'm toying with some possible charges. For one, obstruction of justice," Kelly stated, flatly.

Ettie gasped. "What did she do that you have proof of?"

"I found out she made a call to Ryker, Deena's son. She called his work and left a message, and do you know what that message was?"

Ettie and Elsa-May looked at one another then they looked back at Detective Kelly. "No," they chorused.

"RUN. That's what she said."

"That sounds odd. How do you know that?" Elsa-May asked.

"A fellow from his work played the message for me. It was on Ryker's recorded voice messages at his place of employment in Hazelton, Luzerne County. When I questioned Annie, she admitted it. Now she won't tell me why she told him to run. It makes me think they were in it together."

Ettie cringed at the thought. It wasn't true, Ettie

was sure, but it wasn't sounding great for Annie. "Where is Ryker now?"

"We don't know, thanks to Annie," Kelly snarled.

"Why?" Ettie asked.

"If we were able to find him, we'd have the answer to that. Your friend is remaining tight-lipped. When the body was discovered, Annie knew it wouldn't be long before we traced the evidence to the both of them."

"How long will she be in prison for?" Ettie asked.

"You don't have evidence enough to keep her all this time, do you? Aren't you only supposed to keep her a certain time if she's not arrested for something?"

Ettie winced at Elsa-May's remark. It never went down well when Kelly was questioned in that manner. Thankfully, Kelly didn't seem to hear what Elsa-May said, and answered Ettie's question. "I'm keeping her here for as long as I possibly can, unless she talks."

"Won't she get bail or something? Isn't that the normal process?" Elsa-May asked.

Kelly slowly nodded and his bottom lip curled with irritation. "I'm hoping it won't come to that."

"Can I talk with her?" Ettie asked.

"I'm sorry, but no."

"I might be able to—"

"No!" Kelly raised his voice a notch. "No one can see her right now. Tell me, what information do you have for me?" He looked from one sister to the other.

Ettie shook her head. "Why would she tell him to run?"

"It's obvious. He killed his mother and possibly Annie Lapp knew about it or was an accessory to murder. My theory is, she didn't do the actual killing, but she helped Ryker. She possibly lured Deena to her house and that's why the body was there."

"Why would he kill his own mother? It's not likely." Elsa-May shook her head.

"That reminds me. We have found out something," Ettie said. "Deena is not Ryker's real mother."

Elsa-May said, "I don't think Annie would've done any luring to get—"

"Wait, dial it back a click. What?" Kelly stared at Ettie.

Elsa-May answered before Ettie had a chance. "Not his real mother, that is what Ettie said."

Ettie held up her hand. "Wait, Elsa-May, we don't really know it for certain. I shouldn't have said it unless I knew it was true and I don't. Elsa-May's grandson was a friend of Ryker's and he was told by Ryker that Deena was not his real mother. He claims Deena stole him from his birth parents."

"We also heard it from another person who knew," Elsa-May added.

Kelly waved a hand in the air. "I'm not listening to that hearsay rubbish. Nearly every teenager in America has gotten on the wrong side of their parents and wished they were adopted. Being adopted is a common fantasy. It may be true, but I'd need proof, not just secondhand hearsay from some disgruntled youths. Anyway, it gives more weight to the scenario. If she wasn't his birth mother, he might've resented her."

"Then why would someone bury her on Annie's land?" Elsa-May repeated her unanswered question from a minute ago.

"When your friend starts talking, we'll have more answers." Detective Kelly took out a large handkerchief from his coat pocket and dabbed beads of sweat off his forehead. "Most victims are murdered by people very close to them. In all cases, we look at the immediate family first. More often than not, it's one of them."

"I remember you telling us that some time ago."

He raised his hands in the air. "Nothing's changed, Mrs. Smith. All we have to figure out is exactly where Ryker is. I've got my men on it, but see if you can find out anything else, would you? It would be much appreciated. And keep yourselves out of trouble while you're at it."

"And why Annie told him to," Elsa-May added.

Kelly tipped his head to one side. "Excuse me?"

"We need to find out why Annie told Ryker to run."

Kelly pressed his fingertips together. "I think we can safely say it's because he was guilty, and she knew it. That's the only reason. Something else with Annie Lapp that doesn't add up. She claims to have left a note at her door. There was no note from Annie, in or anywhere near Deena Brown's house!"

Ettie recalled what Annie had said. She'd said she

left a note on the door to tell her about the quilting bee. "Couldn't the note have simply blown away?"

"Or," Elsa-May said, "Someone else could've seen it there and taken it."

Kelly cleared his throat and it came out as more of a growl. "There might be a logical answer, but it doesn't look good for her. Now, for your statement, Mrs. Smith."

"We're looking after Annie's cats. Any idea when she'll be out?" Ettie inquired, knowing she was risking Kelly getting angry.

"If I had my way, it'd be when she talks and no sooner, but I have rules to follow. It's a disappointment when those rules impede our inquiries. Criminals have more rights than they ought."

The sisters stared at him, waiting for what they felt was a proper length of time.

He finally snapped, "She'll be out when she's out."

"Can you tell her we're looking after her animals?"

"I'll let her know, Mrs. Smith."

Ettie saw a pile of folders on his desk. She knew that he kept the coroners reports in a red folder and a red one was on top. "And, might I ask, what was the cause of death?"

"Ah yes." He picked up the red file. "She was struck on the head. It wasn't consistent with a traffic accident, a hit and run—or, as it would've been—a hit, bury and run. No. We have a large rock in evidence and that is confirmed by the coroner to be the murder weapon."

"Oh, that's dreadful." Ettie hung her head. "Does that point to the murder not being planned?"

"Possibly. The report tells me she was struck on the head in the vicinity where she was buried."

"What were the other options?"

Detective Kelly stared at Elsa-May. "Pardon me?"

"What are the other options if Deena hadn't been killed in front of Annie's house?"

"Many people are killed elsewhere and then dumped in some out of the way spot."

"That means somewhere where nobody would go, but she was buried near the roadway right where she died. Why wouldn't they move her body?" Elsa-May asked. "Someone was sure to stumble across it sooner or later."

"I know, it doesn't make a lot of sense," Kelly said. "The body will be released later today."

"Released to whom?" Ettie asked.

"Released to the funeral director per the instructions of your Bishop Paul."

"That's right," Elsa-May said.

"Your bishop said there were no known relatives. He said Deena's husband has been gone for several years. Nobody knows where he is and even if he's still alive."

Ettie blinked rapidly. "Bishop Paul didn't mention that Deena had a son?"

"Yes, but we don't know his whereabouts, so your bishop has taken charge."

"That's kind of him," Ettie mumbled. Or had the bishop taken charge because he knew Ryker wasn't Deena's birth son and he knew they were estranged? They had to talk with the bishop to find out what he knew.

Detective Kelly said, "I can't keep chatting, ladies. I've got things to do. Mrs. Lutz, would you mind waiting outside while Mrs. Smith makes her statement?"

"Of course. I'll wait on one of the seats in the waiting area."

"It shouldn't take too long."

When Elsa-May walked out, Detective Kelly took Ettie to the interview room and set up the recording equipment.

Ettie then repeated everything she remembered.

Afterwards, she walked out and waited with Elsa-May while her statement was printed so she could approve and sign it.

"*Wunderbaar* job, Ettie," Elsa-May said.

"With what?"

"It didn't take ages."

"There wasn't much to say. I saw Deena lying there and the dog running away with the shoe. Then I called Kelly."

"Short and to the point."

"That's the best way. What else would I have said?" Ettie looked down at her hands in her lap.

"For one thing, you could've told them your theory about the note that Annie said was from Deena."

"No one asked me about it. All I did was answer the questions."

Detective Kelly walked down the hallway, smiling at them. "The statement's ready for your signature. You can come back in, Mrs. Smith, and you too, Mrs. Lutz."

They followed Kelly back to his office. Once they were seated, Kelly handed Ettie the statement and she read through it.

"Is it all accurate?" he asked when she looked up.

"Yes."

He passed her a pen. When she had signed it, Kelly thanked her, took the statement and slid it into a folder.

"Now for the funeral. I guess that'll be coming soon." Ettie looked down and shook her head. "It's sad to have a funeral for someone so young with so much life left to live."

He stood up. "Thank you for doing what you can. And again, please keep out of trouble, and don't put yourselves in harm's way."

"We won't."

"I'm thinking Ryker Lapp will be far away by now. We'll find him, though. He won't outsmart us. The way technology is today, it's virtually impossible for someone to disappear without leaving some trace."

Ettie got to her feet and then moved her chair out of the way so Elsa-May could stand.

"Can I have someone drive the two of you home?" he asked.

"No thank you," Elsa-May said. "We have errands to run in town."

He opened his office door for them. "I will look into that story about Ryker Lapp not being the birth son."

Ettie smiled and gave a small nod. On the way down the corridor, Ettie whispered to Elsa-May, "You told him we have errands. What are they?"

Elsa-May's face lit up. "We have an important errand at the café, the one that has those lovely cakes."

Ettie's mouth watered just thinking about the flavorsome baked treats. She looped her arm through Elsa-May's. "I was hoping that's what you meant."

"But we won't stay there long. Just time enough to put some energy into our tanks. We've got to get to the bottom of who killed Deena."

"I agree. From what Mary said, all the ladies in the community are worried too. I do hope they'll let Annie out soon."

CHAPTER 14

When they reached the café, Elsa-May pushed the door open to allow Ettie through first.

"That's nice of you."

"Whoever goes through the door first... well, it's their treat." Elsa-May grinned.

"You mean, it's your treat because you were the first one to touch the door?" Ettie was hopeful, but from the look on her sister's face, Elsa-May wasn't going to agree to that ruling.

"No. Yours."

"I'll pay this time," Ettie said.

"*Jah,* you will." Elsa-May rubbed her tummy. "And that means I just got hungrier."

"That doesn't surprise me, but remember you're supposed to be cutting down on sweets."

Elsa-May pouted. "I remember, and I am cutting down because we haven't been here in ages."

"This is not the only way you have access to sweets and cakes."

Elsa-May frowned at Ettie. "It was a humorous comment, Ettie."

"It wasn't funny, though."

"Never mind. You just didn't understand it. Where was Bishop Paul? He was supposed to be staying at the police station until they released Annie." Elsa-May asked.

"That's right. I didn't see him anywhere."

"He must've left already."

Ettie breathed in the aroma of the freshly ground coffee. "I love this smell."

Elsa-May wasn't listening. She was too busy looking at the array of cakes in the glass display cabinet. "That's a new one there."

Ettie looked to where her sister pointed. "That's just a cupcake. It does look tasty though, but I don't know how I'd eat my way through all that frosting. It's taller than the cake itself. I wonder if those purple flowers are edible."

"Of course they would be, along with the leaves, but I'm not looking at that one. I'm trying to show you the one behind it."

Ettie leaned down further and saw what looked like a fruit cake, and it too had a generous layer of frosting. "It's label says it's a brandy cake."

"Brandy? I can't have it then. I need to keep a level head."

Ettie chuckled. "The alcohol content would've been cooked out of it, leaving only the brandy flavor."

"Still, I'm not going to have it. You decide for me, Ettie. I'll find us a table."

"No, just choose something before you go." Ettie knew that whatever she chose would be wrong, so she wasn't going to fall into that trap again.

Elsa-May flung a hand in the air. "They're each as yummy as the other. Anything will do. Surely I don't have to do everything, do I?"

Ettie pouted. "It's just cake, Elsa-May. And you should choose what you want to eat. How would I know?"

Elsa-May grunted. "I was just trying to get a nice surprise. Fine, just get me a pink cupcake and a cappuccino."

"A pink cupcake it is." Ettie turned away from her sister just as she was approached by the waitress. Ettie chose the lemon meringue pie for herself and the same coffee as her sister.

When Ettie finished paying, she sat down with Elsa-May at their usual table by the window. Being late morning, there were only three other tables occupied. "I do feel awful about sitting here enjoying ourselves when Annie is in a jail cell. Who knows what they're giving her to eat?" Ettie looked down at the metal table, shaking her head.

"Don't worry. They won't starve her. Kelly wouldn't allow that."

"I'm not so sure. It didn't sound that way to me. It sounded like he wanted to beat the information out of her."

"Is that what he meant by the new rules?"

Ettie saw that Elsa-May's eyes were round like saucers. "I don't think so. He probably meant… ach, I don't know *what* he meant. We're doing what we can to help Annie by looking after her animals and trying to find out who did this dreadful thing to Deena."

Elsa-May put her elbows on the table and rested her chin in her hands. "How will we do that when we don't know the first thing about Deena?"

"We know more than you think. She came to the community as a young woman with a *boppli*. She married Hezekiah Lapp."

"But where did she come from?" Elsa-May asked.

"I don't know, but we know her maiden name was Brown."

Elsa-May threw her hands in the air. "Do we even know that, though? How do we know that's for sure true? Besides that, it's not an unusual name so it'll be hard to find out about her past."

"Deena's not the guilty one. Why would she have had anything to hide?"

Elsa-May leaned across the table and hissed, "You're the one who told me Mary said Deena had a secret."

Before Ettie could answer, the waitress brought their drinks and pastries to them on a tray.

Once she left, Elsa-May smiled at her cupcake. "This looks *wunderbaar.*" Her gaze then traveled to Ettie's. "Ach, maybe I should've got one of those."

"We can share. I'll cut mine in half."

"Nee, Ettie." Elsa-May picked up a knife. "I don't trust you to do it fairly. I'll do the cutting. You'll give yourself more. You always do."

Before Ettie could deny it, a knife came down the middle of Ettie's pie, splitting it in two. Without wasting a moment, Elsa-May shoveled one half onto her plate.

Ettie compared the two pieces and was amazed how accurate a job her sister had done, but she wasn't going to give her any praise. "Shall I ask the waitress for a ruler, so we can be sure it's even? Perhaps they have some kitchen scales, too, so we can weigh each section?"

"It's not necessary. I have an eye for measurements." Elsa-May closed one eye and held her tongue between her teeth as she guided the knife right down the center of her cupcake. "There. A clean break. Equal frosting, too."

Ettie smiled. "Very skillful. I was joking about the ruler."

"I know that." Elsa-May lifted one half of the cupcake onto Ettie's plate, sitting it upright next to the half slice of pie.

Ettie picked up her fork. "I'm glad that's over with. Now I hope I can enjoy it, or would you like half my coffee too?"

"I have one of my own. *Denke,* for paying for this Ettie. It was a truly genius idea."

"It was your idea."

"I know." Elsa-May picked up her cappuccino and slurped it.

As always, her slurping grated on Ettie's nerves. "Do you have to do that?" Ettie could only hope that no one else in the café heard it.

"It's hot. When I drink it like that, it slowly cools it to just the right temperature."

"Or, you could wait a while like a normal person would."

"I could've, but I like to alternate the sips of coffee with the bites of cake."

Ettie popped a piece of pie into her mouth. As the tangy lemon mixed with the sweetness of the meringue, she thought about Deena. "To answer your question before the waitress came, you're right. Mary hinted that Deena had a secret. So if she had a secret, it might've been a factor in her murder. We can't rule it out. We'll have to uncover everything we can about her past."

"You think everyone's got secrets, Ettie. This time, though, it might be true."

"It's quite probable."

Elsa-May slurped on her coffee again. "What did Mary say exactly?"

"I don't remember the words she used. I wonder what the secret was. Now I have a knowing deep within myself that Deena had one."

"What do you mean when you say, 'a knowing,' Ettie?"

"When I know something deep down in my heart, that's a knowing."

"It's a new one on me. The secret was probably that Ryker wasn't hers by birth. We already know that. It's not that big a secret. Many folks adopt and don't want the adoptee to know."

"What if the story about her stealing Ryker is true?"

Elsa-May shook her head. "Mary and Bishop Paul wouldn't approve of that."

"*Jah,* you're right, but they might not know. Apart from finding out from Mary or the bishop, where would we go to learn more about her?"

"Oh no." Elsa-May waved a finger at her. "You're not getting me to her *haus*."

"Brilliant, Elsa-May! Her house. We'll go there. We'll be able to find something to take us further along in our knowledge of her. There's bound to be some kind of clue waiting for us."

"There might have been, but don't forget Kelly's already been there. Don't you think that the clue, or any clues, would've stood out to him? Any clues will be closed up tight in his zip-locked plastic bags in the evidence room."

"We just have to hope he missed something." Ettie balanced some pie on her fork.

Elsa-May looked around them, and then whispered, "If we go to Deena's house, we'll be breaking in, is that what you want? You want us to break into her house?"

"It's not really breaking-in. You're making us sound like criminals. What we'll be doing is looking for ways to help Annie and ways to help find who killed poor, Deena." When Elsa-May looked unconvinced, Ettie added, "When you break in, you're breaking in to do bad things. We're not—we're doing something for the good."

"I just hope you don't get caught."

Ettie tipped her head to one side. "Aren't you coming with me?"

"*Nee*. I'm not."

"Pleeease."

Elsa-May shook a dessert fork at Ettie. "Don't look at me like that."

"Please?"

"All right then, but if we go to jail, it'll be all your fault. I'd like to see you try to explain that to your *kinskinner.* And while you're at it, you'll have to explain it to mine, and the bishop."

"I won't have to because we won't get caught. We'll be in and out in no time."

Elsa-May sighed and then she stuck her fork into the bright pink frosting. "*Gott* give me strength."

"Amen, and help us and guide us all the way to helping Deena and our friend, Annie."

"It's too late for Deena," Elsa-May grumbled.

"*Gott* knows what I mean."

"*Jah,* I know, but you've still got to pray using the right words."

"Why?"

"Forget it, Ettie." Elsa-May stared at Ettie while munching on the rest of the half cupcake. "The food's always *wunderbaar* here."

"I know. We'll go to Deena's place now."

Elsa-May shuddered.

"What's wrong?" Ettie asked.

"Don't you remember that Annie said she went there, and it sounded like there was someone in her home? What if someone's hiding there?"

"They would've left by now. Don't forget that Kelly's already been there, and he didn't find anyone hiding." Ettie tapped on her chin. "Come to think of it, he must not have found anything there or he would've told us. So that makes me feel even better about what we're about to do."

"Would he have told us, though? Do you think he tells us everything? He sees us as a couple of old fools who sometimes fall on the truth through luck or happenstance."

"Jah, you're more than likely right about that, but save the big words for your crossword puzzles."

"Doesn't that bother you, Ettie?"

"The word happenstance? It does a little." Ettie took a sip of coffee and put the cup back down on the saucer.

"Nee. I meant that Kelly sees us as silly old fools."

Ettie looked down at her food. "Maybe he sees one of us that way." She looked up at Elsa-May, and quickly added, "What really bothers me is my coffee is cold now."

"That's why you need to eat it along with the cake and not leave it for last."

"Now you tell me—but I do hope you mean *drink* it, not eat it."

"That's what I said, and you're old enough to have figured it out by now. Unless you did and you've forgotten." Elsa-May chortled.

Ettie looked at her coffee. "I can't drink it. I know some people like cold coffee, but I'm not one of them."

"Just leave it. You drank half of it. You don't have to finish it if it's cold."

"Are you ready to go?" Ettie asked.

"Nee. I've still got half a piece of pie left. Half of the half, which is a quarter."

"Ach. Denke for the math lesson."

"You're welcome. Knitting helps me with math. That's why I'm so clever at it. I have to calculate how many skeins I'll need to make an item, and how many stitches for the rows and how many rows will finish a piece."

"Interesting, I'm sure."

"Well, it is. If you applied yourself more to knitting, you'd know that it helps with other areas of life, not only math."

"I would, but I don't enjoy it that much."

"And it shows." Elsa-May tsk tsked.

Ettie wasn't sure where or how it showed, but she had a feeling it was better not to ask. Instead, she pressed her finger on some leftover cake crumbs and then popped them into her mouth. "After this I'm going to Deena's house. You can go home. As Detective Kelly mentioned, we don't have to go everywhere together."

"That's not what he said."

"That's what he meant. So, are you sure you're all right to look around Deena's place? You could go home and I'll go there alone."

Elsa-May groaned. "That's all right. I'll come with you."

"Are you sure you're up to it?"

"I said I was. Stop asking!"

CHAPTER 15

The taxi let Ettie and Elsa-May out at the roadside near Deena's house and the two elderly sisters made their way behind the house, so no one could see them from the road.

"One job's done. We've fed the cats," Ettie said.

"How will we get in? There might be a door, or a window left open. Let's see." Elsa-May tried the back door, but it was locked. Then she took a step to one side, leaned down and looked under the mat. There was no key like there had been at Annie's house.

"Let's try the windows. You go that way and I'll go this way." They went in opposite directions.

On the second window she tried, Ettie was able to lift it up. "Hey, I've got one."

Elsa-May came hurrying to meet her. "Keep your voice down, Ettie. You're yelling so loud they can hear you in China." Then Elsa-May stopped abruptly when she looked at how far the window was above the ground. "How are we supposed to get up there?"

"It's not that far."

"It is. Even on tippy toes we can't heave ourselves up there. What we need is a ladder or something."

Ettie grabbed a branch from the garden and managed to push the window up with it. "There. Easy done."

"Jah, that was, but how can we get in? It won't be so easy."

"We'll do what we did when we were young. You make a foot-hold out of your hands like I'm getting on a tall horse."

"I'll try." Elsa-May interlaced her fingers and lowered her hands for Ettie. Ettie raised her knee, put her boot in Elsa-May's hands and Ettie was boosted through the open window.

"I'm in!" Ettie pulled herself up from the floor, and looked around to see she was in a bedroom.

"Oh dear!" Elsa-May yelled. "There's a horse and buggy coming to the *haus*."

"Oh no. Hide somewhere."

Elsa-May looked around. "There's nowhere except under the house and I'm not going there. This is one of my best dresses."

"It'll be someone come to feed her horses." Ettie leaned out the window as far as she could. "Stand on your tip toes and give me your hand."

"That won't work."

Ettie noticed a small stool in the corner of the room. She passed it out to Elsa-May. "Stand on that, hurry."

Elsa-May wasted no time doing as Ettie suggested and then she grabbed Ettie's hand, and somehow—with Elsa-May moving her feet up the wall and Ettie pulling as hard as she could—Elsa-May made it to the window ledge.

"I'm stuck."

Ettie saw Elsa-May kicking her feet out behind her. She leaned forward and grabbed the back of Elsa-May's dress and pulled her through. Elsa-May ended up on all fours on the floor.

"Ooof."

"Are you all right?"

Elsa-May moved to her knees and dusted off her hands. "I think so. I haven't broken anything."

Not being able to see the buggy from the window, Ettie hurried to the other side of the house. "It's one of the bishop's sons come to feed the horses. I'm so glad they're looking after them." Ettie turned around. Where was Elsa-May? She hurried into the other room and saw Elsa-May still sitting in a heap. "What's the matter?"

"Nothing. I just need a hand. Who's here?"

"The bishop's son, Andrew."

"Oh."

"Don't worry. He'd have no reason to come inside. It looks like he's just here to feed the horses."

"How many does she have? She was living by herself."

"Just the one. Let's not waste time. I'm going to look around."

Ettie took a step away and Elsa-May caught hold of her sleeve. "We'll wait until Andrew leaves. We don't want him to find out we're here."

"Okay. You think he might see us through a window or something?"

"It's possible. We can't risk it. Wait, what if he comes inside?"

"We'll have to hope that he doesn't. If he does, we could say we were looking to see if she had a cat and we were going to feed it, same as we're doing for Annie."

"Ettie," Elsa-May hissed, "that would be a lie."

"Tell him the truth, then."

Elsa-May's mouth turned down at the corners. "We can't do that either."

They both looked out the window and watched Andrew walk into the barn. Then he came out with an armful of hay and tossed it over the fence to the horse and then went into the barn again.

"He's taking a long time," Ettie said.

"Shh."

"He can't hear me."

"You're giving me a headache, Ettie."

Then they saw him coming out of the barn with something covered in a dark gray blanket, tied with rope. Elsa-May dug Ettie in the ribs. "What's that?"

Ettie rubbed her side and moved away. "How would I know?"

"It's long and narrow."

Ettie gasped. "Could it be a body? Hezekiah's body? Maybe he didn't just disappear. Maybe he was killed."

"*Nee,* Ettie. It's too light. Look how he's carrying it."

They moved from that room to one that was closer to Andrew. He put whatever it was down on the ground so he could open the buggy door at the back. Then he picked it up and put it in his buggy, closing the door once he'd finished.

"It looks heavy whatever it is. Not as heavy as a body, I guess."

"I can't even imagine what it would be and why he'd be taking it away," Elsa-May said.

"Maybe Mary will know. She must've asked him to come here to feed the horse."

Elsa-May grabbed Ettie's shoulder. "What's he doing? He's not getting in the buggy."

"You're right. He's not."

"He's coming this way."

Ettie looked around. They were in the living room. There were two couches and right where they stood, they were between a two-seater couch and the window. "We'll have to hide."

"Where?"

"Here."

At that moment, they heard the door open and Ettie grabbed Elsa-May and pulled her down with her.

They both huddled behind the couch.

CHAPTER 16

After a moment, Ettie and Elsa-May heard the front door of Deena's house close and then echoing footsteps were heard walking into the room.

"Hello. Anybody here? Hello?"

Ettie and Elsa-May froze as they huddled in their hiding place.

Did he know they were there?

Had he seen them?

Elsa-May stared at Ettie, who shook her head and put her finger up to her mouth signaling for her not to make a sound.

Elsa-May then shut her eyes tightly while Ettie held her breath.

Then the steps echoed into the kitchen, giving a tapping sound as he walked onto the linoleum flooring. They heard cupboard doors opening and closing. Then

Andrew walked from the kitchen, across the living room where they were, and headed to the bedrooms.

"Hello. Anyone here?"

Again, Elsa-May gave Ettie a questioning look asking if they should show themselves.

Ettie shook her head.

How could they?

Two grown women hiding in a house?

And, a house where they hadn't been invited?

It would be unthinkably embarrassing.

Then they heard the front door open and then close. After they heard the boards on the porch creak, Ettie raised her head. She whispered, "He's leaving, I hope."

Elsa-May raised her head, and on her knees looked out the window. "I do hope he didn't know we were in here. What if he'd seen us get out of the taxi?"

"It wasn't us. He was looking for someone else, don't you see?"

"No." Elsa-May took hold of the back of the couch and pulled herself up, and Ettie did the same. "Why do you say that?"

"Remember what Annie thought?"

Elsa-May ran her hands down her dress to smooth it out. "I'm sorry, but I don't place much store on what Annie says anymore. I heard it, but I thought she was making the whole thing up because she was bored, or because she wanted to have something to talk about."

"What if she wasn't mistaken, and wasn't making it

up? She thought someone was here and it can't have been Deena because she was already dead."

Elsa-May scratched her cheek.

Ettie went on to explain, "Andrew also expected someone to be here it seems. Why?"

Elsa-May's eyes opened wide. "Ettie, if someone has been here that means they might be coming back."

Ettie gasped and covered her mouth. "I didn't even think of that."

Elsa-May leaned forward and whispered, "What if they're in here right now hiding in a cupboard. Hiding from us and from Andrew?"

Ettie bolted for the front door, leaving Elsa-May to follow at a slightly slower pace. When there was no sign of Elsa-May, Ettie stepped back inside the house and hissed, "Come on."

"Wait! I found something in the kitchen. Come here."

A jolt went through Ettie's body. They'd gone there to find something and she'd allowed herself to be distracted by Andrew taking something out of the barn. Ettie followed Elsa-May's voice to the kitchen.

Spread out on the table was a jigsaw puzzle.

Ettie looked down at it. "Is this what you're talking about?"

Elsa-May looked up at Ettie smiling. "She was doing the exact same puzzle as the one she gave me."

"Hmm. I wonder how many years it takes to do this one." Ettie picked up the lid and turned it over. It still had the price tag on it. "Look at this. It comes from a toy store at Hazelton, Luzerne County. It says so in small writing on the price sticker."

"That's funny, isn't it?"

Ettie put the lid back where she found it. "I guess she went there once." Ettie looked around. "Kelly said this place was trashed. They must've put it back together."

"Who did?"

"The police when they were looking through it for evidence."

The sisters left the kitchen and just as Ettie touched the front door, a van pulled up. She quickly closed the door and leaned against it.

"Make up your mind. Are we going or are we staying? Coming or going?" Elsa-May asked.

"Shh. Someone else is here."

Elsa-May's eyebrows flew up so high they nearly reached her prayer *kapp*. "Who?"

"I don't know. Quick, into the bedroom."

They hurried into the bedroom and then Ettie peeped out the window.

"What do you see?" Elsa-May crouched on the floor next to the window.

"A man. I'd say he'd be about fifty or so."

"Is he coming into the house?" Elsa-May asked.

"He's going into the barn. His van has something written on the side. Use your glasses to see if you can make it out."

"They're only for close up."

"Just try."

Elsa-May un-looped her glasses from the top of her dress. She put them on and then stood up and looked out. "No. I told you they wouldn't work. I can't see past the window."

Ettie snatched them off her face. "Give them here." Ettie put them on, and then she took them off and held them up to her eyes, backward. "I can make out the words. Amish Diner, it looks like."

"Oh, that van belongs to Amish Dinner. It could be Mr. Thripp."

"Amish Dinner doesn't make sense. It must be Amish Diner."

"Ettie, there is no diner. Trust me, it's called Amish Dinner. Give back my spectacles, now."

Ettie handed them over and then stared out the window. "What is a man from an Amish diner doing here?"

"He's from Amish Dinner, and Wayne mentioned him, said he'd be upset about Deena."

"I remember now. He must've been a friend of hers."

When Ettie saw the short balding man coming out of the barn, she pulled her sister down to the floor with her. "I just hope he doesn't come in here, too."

"I don't think he will. He might've been in the barn looking for whatever Andrew took out of it just now."

When they heard the rattling of the front doorknob,

they both looked at each other and must've been thinking the same thing because they both made their way under the bed.

They lay in the cramped space amongst the dust for the next five minutes while they listened to the man walking through the house, opening and closing cupboards, and moving things about.

"He's looking for something," Ettie whispered.

"Shh. Unless you want to get us both killed."

"You shh."

Then they both had to be extra quiet because the footsteps stopped and then they got louder, closer. From their hiding place, they saw the bottom half of him entering the room. He proceeded to open the two closet doors. Ettie hoped he wouldn't look under the bed. Just as she thought that, her nose tickled from the dust. She daren't not move a muscle to put her hand up to rub her nose.

Then she felt Elsa-May move and she looked over to see tears coming from her eyes and her face screwed up. She was trying hard not to sneeze as well. And it was no wonder. They were lying in a sea of dust.

Then the man spoke. "Deena, are you here? I just want to tell you I'm sorry. I'm truly sorry. I hope you can hear me from wherever you are."

Ettie's heartbeats quickened. He's sorry, so he must be the killer. He had to be. She closed her eyes tightly and prayed that he wouldn't find out they were there, or he might kill them, too.

"Deena, If you're still here give me some kind of a sign."

Ettie's nose tickled and she couldn't move to scratch it, so she wiggled it about hoping the urge to sneeze would go away.

"Please do your best to communicate with me. I know it might be hard for you since you're newly crossed over, but just make some kind of sound, anything."

Ettie could no longer hold it in and the sneeze left her body as a loud, high-pitched squeak.

The man let out an ear-piercing yell, and ran out of the house.

Ettie froze. She'd never heard a man scream like that, but she was delighted he was gone.

The next thing they heard was his van's engine revving up. Then, the van zoomed down the driveway.

Ettie and Elsa-May made their way out from under the bed, and as soon as they stood, Elsa-May sneezed.

Then they looked at each other and laughed. Ettie laughed so hard her legs got weak and she lowered herself to the floor.

Elsa-May sat on the bed, holding her stomach. When she stopped chortling, she said, "He thought you were a ghost, Ettie. He thought you were Deena reaching out to him."

Ettie did her best to stop laughing. "Just as well, or he would've found us. How embarrassing would that have been—two old ladies hiding under a bed?" Ettie reached her hands up and Elsa-May helped her to her feet.

"I've never heard anyone move so fast. He could win a race with his speediness." Then the smile left Elsa-May's face. "We'll have to hope he doesn't come back. We should leave now before he realizes what he heard was no ghost."

"*Jah*. Good idea."

"We could've been the next victims, Ettie. A fine mess you've dragged me into. Should I say, *another* fine mess?"

Ettie frowned and looked out the window. "We've got to get home somehow, and fast before we get more visitors. It's been quite a busy place."

"Stop staring at that horse. I'm not riding it and neither are you. And if we take Deena's buggy, we'd be stealing and besides, we have nowhere to put either the horse or the buggy when we get home."

"I wasn't looking at the horse. I was wondering if she has a phone in her barn. I'm too old to even think about riding a horse. I'm too scared to go in the barn. You go and look for one."

Elsa-May's mouth dropped open. "I certainly will not!"

Ettie sighed. "This is dreadful. We'll have to walk and hope the man from the Amish diner doesn't come back."

"Amish Dinner," Elsa-May corrected.

"There's a public telephone about two miles in that

direction." Ettie walked out of the house. Then she turned around when she saw her sister wasn't following. "Come on."

Elsa-May raised her left foot. "I can't walk two miles. These are new shoes. I'll get blisters. You know how my feet are oddly slim. It takes ages for the leather to soften and it'll be rubbing on my sensitive skin." Elsa-May hung her head. "I'll go into the barn. If *Gott* is gracious, there will be a phone."

That was the best news Ettie had heard all day. "I'll stay here and keep watch." While Elsa-May walked into the barn, Ettie got ready to join her in the barn if the man came back.

When Elsa-May returned, smiling, a few minutes later, Ettie knew she'd found a phone in the barn. "We have a taxi coming," Elsa-May announced.

"*Wunderbaar.* Now your skinny feet don't have to walk."

"We should wait down by the roadside."

"I'll agree with you on that, but not so much about your feet being slim."

"They are. You shouldn't mock me, Ettie. I've had them measured the last time I went to buy boots. They said my feet are narrow and that's why I've always had ill-fitting shoes."

Ettie stopped herself from saying that Elsa-May's feet were the only narrow things about her.

Once they were down by the road, Ettie said, "Did you see any clue in the barn as to what Andrew took?"

Elsa-May shook her head. "How could I get a clue about something that wasn't there?"

Ettie bit her lip realizing how silly her question was.

"No, I didn't. We'll go directly to Mary's house. She'll know why the bishop wasn't at the police station. Hopefully, we'll find out a lot more, too."

"Agreed."

CHAPTER 17

When Ettie and Elsa-May arrived at the bishop's house, they found that only Mary was home. She showed them into the living room where they sat with hot tea and freshly baked pumpkin cookies.

Mary said, "It's a funny thing that Deena's son has gone missing. I even called the place where he worked and they haven't heard from him. He didn't show up for work on the day Deena's body was found, and they said he's not answering his phone."

"That is odd."

"*Jah,* it is. I'm wondering, Mary, if we should feed Deena's horse or do anything at her *haus?*" Ettie asked, trying to find out some information.

"Nee, don't you worry yourselves. Andrew is taking care of that."

"What is he doing, exactly?" Elsa-May asked.

"Just whatever needs to be done. I'm quite concerned and so are the ladies. They are worried about what happened to Deena happening again—to one of them. We're going to organize a ladies meeting."

"Mary, I'll come straight to the point. Who do you think wanted to harm Deena?" Elsa-May asked.

Mary immediately looked down. "How would I know?"

Ettie took over. "Yesterday you hinted at a secret. Deena had a secret, I'm sure of that. Was it to do with her past? Has someone from her past killed her, do you think?"

"I shouldn't say anything."

"You should, Mary."

"When she came to us, she was in trouble. She told us she'd changed her name to Deena Brown and she said she and the boy needed a new start. When we were in the midst of finding somewhere for her and her son to live, she married Hezekiah. It was so sudden it took us all by surprise."

"I remember their wedding," Elsa-May said.

Mary kept talking, "By the time she married, she'd been baptized and had taken the instructions." After a deep breath, Mary added, "We thought all her problems were over."

"So, she was running away from something or someone?"

"I can't say any more. I've said too much already."

"We're only trying to help."

"That's right. Help Annie get out of jail. We all know she didn't have anything to do with it."

"Paul is back there today, appealing to the police and doing everything he can to get Annie released. There's nothing more I can tell you."

Ettie looked at Elsa-May. "We were at the station earlier and didn't see him."

"He might've gone to get a bite to eat. He left here early, before breakfast."

"Mary, what do you know about the man from the Amish Dinner?"

"Nothing. Why?"

"We saw his van at her house when we were passing just now."

Mary looked down into her teacup. After she raised it to her lips and took a sip, she said, "It was most likely Mr. Thripp, if he was a middle-aged man. He's the owner of the Amish Dinner. He collected things she made for the store, and that's all. There were rumors, but then there are always rumors. People do like to speculate."

"That's true, there always are rumors. We should go, Elsa-May. We've hardly been home and Snowy needs to be let out."

"I'll have Andrew take you home. He's around here somewhere."

"Don't bother him. We'll go home by taxi."

"I can't let you do that. I'll see if Andrew can do it."

"I think we saw him when we were being driven here. His buggy was going in the other direction. Might we borrow your phone to call the taxi company?"

"Of course you can. I'd take you home myself, but our second buggy is being repaired right now."

"Elsa-May, you make the call, would you?"

Elsa-May looked down at her feet. "I would do it, but I fear I'm getting blisters. The less I walk in these new shoes, the better off I'll be."

Ettie stood. "I'll do it then."

Five minutes later, the two elderly sisters walked down the driveway to wait for the taxi at the roadside. "You'll never guess what Mary told me just now when you left to make the phone call," Elsa-May said.

Ettie looked down at the basket in Elsa-May's hands. "What's that you're carrying?"

"Cake. She baked too many this morning and she forced me to take it."

"That's nice. We can have some after dinner and we now have something to offer visitors. We haven't had time to bake these last few days."

"Did you hear what I said, Ettie?"

Ettie thought back. "She told you something, you said, what was it?"

"That's right. She told me something Deena told Annie in confidence. Deena was in this community hiding from a man."

"What man?" Ettie asked.

"A man from many years ago who didn't want her to

leave him. A dangerous kind of a man. It was an ex-boyfriend. She never knew his name because Deena never said."

"I don't like the sound of that. Why would Deena tell Annie and not tell Mary?"

"I'm not sure. The only one who knows that for sure is Deena and we can't ask her, no matter what Mr. Thripp thinks?"

Ettie frowned at her sister. "What are you talking about?"

"Mr. Thripp thinks he can talk to the dead."

Ettie laughed. "He does, too. So this man… he didn't want her to leave him?"

"I guess that's right."

"Do you think all these years later the man took revenge? It doesn't seem likely I suppose. It wouldn't have taken that long to find her and surely he would've been over it with all this time that has passed."

"What makes you think you know that, Ettie? You have to say you know everything, but you can't possibly know everything. I've just given you some interesting information and you completely discount it as useless. Is that because Mary didn't tell you and you didn't find out straight from her? Are you jealous that Mary confided in me about what she heard?"

"*Nee!* It just doesn't make sense. If this mystery man was so upset with her, wouldn't he have done something before now?"

"How do you know he wasn't looking for her for all this time, Ettie? He might have been."

"What else did Mary say?"

Elsa-May smiled so widely all the skin on her cheeks creased with deep lines. "We talked about shoes. And would you believe it? She has slim feet as well."

"What a coincidence," Ettie said.

"I know. It's very rare, and we both have problems with our feet slipping around in our shoes."

"That's easy solved. Just wear a second pair of socks."

Gone was Elsa-May's smile. "Don't you think if it was that easy I would've thought of it? No, that's right because you have to be the one to think of everything, don't you?"

"That's right," Ettie wasn't listening. After spending years with Elsa-May she'd learned the art of the automatic reply.

"Did you hear me?" Elsa-May asked.

"That's right. Here's the taxi. Don't say a word until we get home. We don't want to be overheard."

"I won't say a thing."

Fifteen minutes later, Ettie was glad to be home. She pushed the door open ahead of Elsa-May and Snowy ran to them.

"Ettie, you put the teakettle on, and I'll take him out the back."

"Sure."

"And do we have enough leftovers from last night's dinner?"

"I think we do."

"We might have to cook a few more potatoes."

"I'll check." Ettie headed to the kitchen, happy to be thinking about simple everyday things.

CHAPTER 18

The next day, the sisters had still heard nothing from the detective and didn't know if Annie would be released today or whether she'd been officially arrested.

"I'm bothered by the man from Amish Dinner, who thought I was a ghost," Ettie said. "What was his connection to Deena and why was he saying he was sorry unless he killed her? I think he's got to be the killer."

"*Nee,* Ettie. He could've been sorry about any number of things."

"Hmm. Why don't we find out what we can about him from Wayne? He knows a lot about Deena. He certainly seems to be the one who spent the most time with her in the last days of her life. Then after we talk to him, we'll feed Annie's cats if she's not home."

"Okay. I do hope Annie comes home soon, so I

won't have to see or smell another cat tray as long as I live." Elsa-May pulled a disgusted face.

ONCE AGAIN, Wayne showed the sisters into his small, dark living room, and they sat down. Elsa-May and Ettie were on a small couch and Wayne sat in his old, worn-out chair beside them. "Would you like water?" he asked them.

"We're fine, but thanks," Elsa-May answered. "Where's Snowy today?"

"Out and about. I can't keep him home." He eyed them both. "Don't believe the rumors about me. They're not true, any of them."

Ettie wondered why he wouldn't open the curtains to let in some light. "What rumors?"

"The one about me and Deena. Isn't that why you're here?"

"No!" Elsa-May said. "We're here to ask you about the Amish Dinner."

"About the owner of the Amish Dinner and Deena?" he asked.

"Dinner and Deena. That has a nice sing-song sound." Elsa-May looked up at the ceiling, smiling.

Ettie frowned at her sister. They had to stick to the reason they were there.

"The rumors aren't true about Deena and him either," he said. "Deena was still a married woman and

Mr. Thripp was a married man. Deena earned a little money by making things for his store. He picked them up personally and that's where the rumors started."

"How is that rumor-worthy?" Ettie asked.

"I can't tell you that. All I know is that there was talk. I didn't like it and neither did Deena, but some people have nothing more to do than look for drama hoping for a scandal of some kind. Mr. Thripp asked her to work in his store and she did for a time."

Ettie pressed her back into the couch, trying to get more comfortable. "I didn't know that."

"Yes. It's true. He had her working there and after several days, said he didn't need her anymore. She was upset. Some of the staff said she talked people out of buying things. But she told me she was just giving them the right advice. I said she did the right thing. You can't sell something just to make the money if it doesn't suit the purpose."

Elsa-May frowned. "But aren't we just talking about pickles and jams? I can't see she'd have to be a high-pressure saleswoman, or tell lies to sell those. They should sell themselves."

He shrugged his shoulders. "I can't tell you what I don't know. And that's all I know because it's what she told me."

"She was fired from her job?" Ettie asked.

"That's right, but Mr. Thripp still stopped by to collect the pickles and the produce that she made. *Jah*, they were friends and that probably wasn't a good idea because people were talking. I told her and she laughed it off. I can see her smiling face now." He sighed.

"How often would he visit her?" Ettie asked.

He stared at Ettie for a while before he answered. "Now don't go thinking there was anything to it because there wasn't."

"I'm not thinking anything. It's just a question."

He moved his jaw around as though he was trying to keep his dentures in place. "Maybe two or three times a week. I'd collect her at two to work at my place and bring her home about five. Often, he'd be waiting for her. I'd help her with her horses and such and he'd just sit and wait in his car like he didn't have anywhere more important to be. It seemed a waste of time."

"What did Deena say about it?"

"Just that he was collecting the produce. I know you're thinking she could've left off and given him the goods and then he could've been on his way, but she said he didn't mind waiting."

"And when you'd helped Deena with her work, you'd leave her there with Mr. Thripp?"

"That's right. I didn't want to stay around like I was watching her or checking up on her. She was an independent woman, and if I'd done that, she would've thought I didn't trust her."

"So you did trust her?"

"I trust everyone until they give me reason not to."

Elsa-May leaned forward. "Some say that trust should be earned."

"I don't agree. For me, trust is given until it's abused. No one has ever let me down."

Ettie smiled. "I like your thinking."

"That's all very well, but surely some discretion should be used," Elsa-May said. "You can't go around trusting everyone."

"I can't tell you how to live and I can't tell anyone else how, either. I just know what feels right to me."

Ettie studied him for a moment, wondering if he ever drove out to check how long Mr. Thripp stayed on these regular visits. She didn't have the heart to inquire.

Elsa-May must've been thinking along the same lines. "So, he'd collect the items for his store and then leave?"

"I don't know. He might've stayed for a refreshment. I never asked and she never told me. As I said, I trusted her and she never gave me a reason to doubt her."

"I hope you don't mind us asking you all these questions, Wayne."

"I've got nothing to hide, Ettie."

"I know you don't, but someone has something to hide and Ettie and I are trying to find out who it is. Ettie wants to get to the bottom of who killed Deena."

"It won't bring her back, Ettie."

"I'm aware of that, but it might stop it happening to someone else. The women in the community are quite fearful. Some of them think someone might be targeting them."

His eyes bugged out. "Are they?"

"The detective we've been talking to doesn't think there's any reason to believe that."

"I'll miss Deena. She was a wonderful woman."

Ettie and Elsa-May exchanged looks.

Elsa-May said, "Do you remember her son?"

"I do remember Ryker, but Deena and I weren't very friendly with each other back when he was around. She was married when he was young and then Hezekiah left. It took some years until we developed a friendship. Two lonely souls coming together by *Gott's* grace. We were thinking Hezekiah must've died. If he hadn't died somewhere, he would've come back home."

Ettie was sure she could cross Wayne off her suspect list, and she hoped Detective Kelly would do the same.

"Did she ever talk about her son?" Elsa-May asked.

He rubbed his chin and his gaze traveled to the ceiling. "Not often."

"And why do you think that was?"

"It caused her too much pain because he left the community. He'd got off the narrow way to chase the pleasures of the world. What parent wouldn't be sad about that?"

"That's true enough," Ettie said. "I have two of my own who've left and they don't look like they'll ever return. It does cause me worry and has given me some sleepless nights."

"And Deena wouldn't have been any different. So, have you thought of someone who might wish her harm?" Elsa-May asked.

He shook his head. "No one I can think of."

"What about the man who owned the Amish Diner? You don't know much about him. Do you think he would have any reason to—"

"It's dinner, Ettie. The Amish Dinner," Elsa-May grumbled.

"That's what I said."

Elsa-May huffed. "Nee, you said diner."

"I know what you mean, Ettie. I don't know. He seemed like a trustworthy man for an *Englisher.* Deena never said a mean word about him. And, now that you mention it, I never heard a mean or a cross word about anybody come out of her lips."

Ettie marveled that he could see such a different side of the woman, compared to the one Ryker had portrayed to her grandnephew. But Wayne only saw her for a few hours a day. Ryker had lived with her. The other explanation could've been that one of them was lying.

Several minutes later, they headed to the taxi Wayne had called for them.

Elsa-May grumbled, "I'm glad we're going home. My feet hurt."

"*Nee,* Elsa-May, we're not going home. Didn't we agree we'd go to the Amish Dinner?"

"My feet are killing me. We'll go tomorrow."

"We have to go now. You always say never put off to tomorrow what you can do today."

Elsa-May sighed. "How about we go home, I'll change my shoes and then we'll go out again?"

Ettie was relieved they'd come up with a compromise. "That suits me. First, we must stop and feed the cats."

Elsa-May sighed. "If we must."

CHAPTER 19

Later that day when they were at home and just about to leave for the Amish Dinner, a car pulled up right outside their house.

As it happened, Ettie had been looking out the window at the time. "Elsa-May, a car has just stopped outside our house. Two people are getting out. A man and a woman. The man was driving."

"How old are they?"

"I would say they're in their fifties. They are fairly well dressed and their car doesn't look very old. It's white and glossy, so shiny it must be new."

"Are they coming to the door?"

Ettie moved back so they wouldn't be able to see her and then looked out. "Yes."

"Most likely they want to have a look through the house next door. I can't think of any other reason they'd be here."

"*Jah,* I think so. Grab the keys." Ettie moved to the door, flung it open and was faced with the couple walking up the two front porch steps. "Hello."

"Hello." The man pointed to the house next door. "We'd like to have a look through if we could. The notice we saw in town said to ask at this house for the key."

Elsa-May pushed Ettie out of the way. "Good morning. I have the key. I'll show you through."

The man didn't flinch. All he did was hold his hand out for the key. "There's no need. We'll show ourselves and return the key when we're done."

"I don't mind at all. In fact, I insist."

"No, we'd rather..."

It was too late. Elsa-May had pushed passed them and was out the garden gate.

The couple started walking after her, so Ettie closed the front door.

"Are you moving to the area?" Ettie asked when she'd caught up.

"Yes, we're thinking about it. And this seemed a cheap house compared to the others we've seen."

"And where are you from?" asked Ettie.

"We're from Hazelton."

Elsa-May stopped still, and turned around to face them. "Hazelton in Luzerne County?"

"Yes."

Elsa-May stared at them.

"What's wrong with that?" the wife asked.

"Nothing. It's just that we've heard of Hazelton more times over the last few days than we have our entire lifetimes."

The man cleared his throat, and said nothing. Elsa-May turned around and kept walking.

"It's a lovely house," Ettie said as soon as they stood at the front door.

"We'll soon see." The woman stood back and studied the exterior. "It looks a little drab on the outside, but we do like the area. It seems lovely and quiet."

Elsa-May placed the key in the lock and turned it. "As you can see, it opens onto the living room, which is spacious and there's a lovely fireplace over there, which has been recently cleaned and it's in good working order." She took two steps toward the kitchen and turned around. "The electricity has been de-wired because we had some guests of our community staying here, but I'm sure it's no problem to have it re-wired again."

Ettie said, "The owner said he'll have that done included in the price."

The man put his hands on his hips and looked around. "That doesn't concern us. It won't take much to do that."

"Now through here is the kitchen." Elsa-May stepped into the kitchen. "As you can see, it's a decent size, large cupboards, and plenty of countertop space."

"It's okay, we can have a look through ourselves," the man said.

"We'd prefer that," his wife added.

Elsa-May stared at them with raised eyebrows. "My sister and I will wait outside, then."

"Thank you."

Elsa-May and Ettie headed out the door and Elsa-May folded her arms and tapped the toe of her boot on the ground. "That was rude of them. I was only trying to help."

"You didn't have to state the obvious all the time. They could see that the living room was the living room and that the kitchen was... well, a kitchen."

Elsa-May pushed out her lips. "I was just trying to be friendly."

"Some people don't appreciate friendliness."

"Do you want them as neighbors?" Elsa-May folded her arms across her chest.

Ettie shrugged. "It's not our choice to make. Gabriel has to sell it to someone."

"Yeah, but if you could choose, would you want people as rude as them living next to you?"

"Probably not," Ettie said.

"I shall tell him to leave."

Ettie grabbed hold of Elsa-May's arm. "Nee, we can't lose the sale for our dear friend. He might need the money."

"I didn't think of that."

"They might be better neighbors than some."

"Or worse than others." Elsa-May chuckled.

The potential buyers appeared at the door. "Thank you. We've finished now."

Elsa-May smiled at them. "What do you think?"

"It's a lot smaller than we're used to."

"But it's affordable and I do like the kitchen space. Of course, it will need modernizing to bring it to our standards," the wife said. "But we'll have money to do all the renovations and do it how we want it."

"It's a bit dusty." The husband dusted off his hands. "We'll think about it."

"Yes, it's best to take a while to think about things to make sure you don't make a mistake," Elsa-May told them. "You do know that a murder took place here, don't you?"

The woman's mouth fell open and she clutched her husband's arm. "No."

"It wasn't a bad murder," Ettie said, "and they found the killer, so no need to worry."

The man patted his wife's hand. "That explains the price."

Elsa-May smiled. "That's right, but it's a bargain if that kind of thing doesn't bother you, or if it doesn't happen again."

Ettie couldn't believe Elsa-May's words, and the couple didn't look happy.

"You could've told us that before we went inside," the woman snapped.

"Come on, dear." The man grabbed his wife's hand

and they hurried past the sisters and continued to their car.

Ettie and Elsa-May stood and watched them leave.

"Well, they're not going to be our neighbors," Ettie finally said. "Such a shame."

"I'll make sure all the doors and windows are locked. You can't be too careful with what's happened around here."

While Elsa-May went through the house, Ettie stayed and watched the couple drive away. When Elsa-May returned, Ettie said, "We didn't even get their name or their phone number. Were we supposed to do that?"

Elsa-May shrugged her shoulders. "Gabriel didn't say. And, it's funny that they didn't introduce themselves."

"But, neither did we."

"We can't worry about that now. It's off to the Amish Dinner."

"Great. I am hungry."

"Eat before you go. I keep telling you it's not a diner and they don't serve food."

Ettie sighed. "I meant... never mind."

"Let's not discuss it again." Elsa-May shook her head.

CHAPTER 20

An hour later, the elderly sisters arrived at Amish Dinner.

"I can't believe that we've just discovered this place. Look at all these things." Ettie picked up a jar of pickled pears. "I don't think I've ever tasted pickled pears. They look delightful."

Elsa-May whispered, "We're not here for new taste sensations or for our stomachs. We're here to see what we can find out about Mr. Thripp."

Ettie put the jar back on the shelf. "I know, but there's no harm in looking while we're here. I don't know how you've been here and I haven't."

"I can't help that."

Ettie said, "I'll keep my eyes open, but he doesn't seem to be here. I can't see him anywhere." Ettie sensed someone standing close to her. She turned around to see the woman who'd been through the house next door.

"Hello again," the woman said.

"Hello."

Elsa-May turned around and saw her, too. "Nice to see you again."

The woman said, "You might see us about. We're staying until we buy a place."

"I hope you're considering the house next to us? It's a lovely peaceful area and you did say you're looking for somewhere quiet."

The husband came around the corner. "Ah, hello again."

"Ralf, these are the ladies from that house we saw this morning. They asked if we're considering it. What do you think?"

"It's not out of the question. It's on our short list, but only because of the price."

"If you say so." Elsa-May nodded. "I'm Elsa-May and this is my sister, Ettie."

"Nice to meet you for the second time. I'm Ralf and this is my wife, Madeline."

"Call me Maddie, everyone does. Out of interest, do you know the Amish lady who owns this place?"

"No, it's a man who owns it," Ettie said. "And he's not Amish. His name is Mr. Thripp."

"I heard an Amish woman owns it. We've been customers here for over a year now. We buy from their website and we couldn't wait to get here and look at all the goodies in person."

"We came here the day we arrived and we overheard someone talking about the owners. I'm sure they said it was an Amish woman and a man."

"An Amish man?" Ettie asked.

"No, just a man."

"We know the man who owns it," Elsa-May said.

Ettie regretted her sister saying that. It could come back to bite them. "We don't know him well, but we know he's Mr. Thripp. We do know that no Amish woman owns it. If one did, we'd know."

"I see. We must've heard wrong, then." Maddie looked at her husband, who just continued to stare at Elsa-May and Ettie. Maddie then looked down at the end of the store. "Oh, look, Ralf. It's Mrs. Thripp. I recognize her from the website. We must say hello and tell her how much we like her store."

"So you know the store is owned by the Thripps?" Ettie asked.

"We thought so, at least, along with the Amish woman."

"Sorry to bother you again," Ralf said, taking a step back.

"You're not bothering us," Elsa-May told them.

They smiled, and then Maddie said, "We might see you again soon."

Once they were gone, Elsa-May dug Ettie in the

ribs. "Why would they think an Amish woman owns this place? Is that what it says on the internet?"

Ettie rubbed her side. "I don't know. I've never looked. They seemed so much nicer just now."

"And where is Mr. Thripp?"

"I don't know."

"Ettie, what's wrong with you? You see a bottle of pickled pears and your brain goes to mush. Do I have to do everything?"

"You don't have to do everything." Ettie took the jar of pickled pears off the shelf. "But I will hold onto this one because it is the last one."

"I had to clean the cat trays and put out the kibble while you sat on Deena's couch, pondering. On the first day, you said you were going to do the trays the next day. Annie will be home soon and you'll have missed out on cleaning even one tray."

Ettie sighed. "Will it make you happy if I buy a cat tray and clean it? Perhaps we'll teach Snowy to use it so I can clean it as many times as you did."

"At least it would be fair." Elsa-May pouted.

"We could always get a cat. I've been thinking about that for a while."

Elsa-May shook her head. "It would be awful for Snowy. He'd get less attention."

"He wouldn't notice. He spends half the day asleep anyway."

"The house is too small." Elsa-May screwed up her nose.

Ettie whispered, "We should talk with Mrs. Thripp since Mr. Thripp doesn't appear to be here. Now that we're here, we have to ask someone some questions."

They both moved to the next aisle and saw a middle-aged woman talking to the couple who'd visited next door.

"That must be her. We never knew there was a Mrs. Thripp."

"We did, Ettie. Wayne said Mr. Thripp was a married man."

"*Jah,* he did, didn't he? I wonder if she too heard the rumors about her husband and Deena."

"Why don't you ask her?" Elsa-May smiled at her own sarcastic comment.

"I guess we could. I didn't think of that."

"I was joking."

"How else would we find out?"

"Oh, Ettie, you can't walk up to someone and ask her something personal like that."

"I can."

"What I mean is, she might think her husband was in love with Deena, and she might've been the killer. You'll be inflaming the situation."

"*Jah,* I suppose."

"Jealousy is a good motive for murder, they say." Elsa-May blinked rapidly.

"Who says so?" Ettie asked.

"I heard it somewhere. Love, money and jealousy. I think love and jealousy are combined."

Ettie nodded, as though she agreed. It was easier that way.

They kept watching until the couple moved away and Mrs. Thripp was left on her own. The sisters approached her as she was trying to fix a hand-held machine.

She looked up at them. "Hello, can I help you ladies?"

Ettie looked at the machine in Mrs. Thripp's hands. "It looks like you're the one who needs help."

Mrs. Thripp smiled. "Oh this? It's our price-tag machine. My husband is the only one who can get the silly thing to work and he's not here at the moment."

"So, you're Mrs. Thripp?" Ettie asked.

"I am."

Elsa-May said, "We have heard that an Amish woman owns this store, and we've also heard your husband does, so we're just..."

The smile left Mrs. Thripp's face. "We're an Amish grocery store, so people naturally assume there's an Amish owner, but they're wrong."

"We know Deena Brown, the woman who used to work here."

Mrs. Thripp sighed. "Oh yes. I heard about her recent... death. It was very sad."

"How did you hear?" Ettie asked.

"It's all over the news. Everyone's talking about it."

"I believe the police spoke to your husband."

"And maybe yourself," Ettie added.

Mrs. Thripp's eyebrows drew together. "What's this about? Why are you here asking these things? You must already know Deena worked here once." She looked them up and down. "I don't remember seeing either of you here before."

"We're here to buy pickled pears for my sister," Elsa-May said, smiling.

"I'll show you where they are."

Ettie lifted up the bottle in her hands. "I got the last one."

"Yes, lucky last. These are so popular we can barely keep them on the shelves."

"I didn't think pickled pears would be so popular," Elsa-May said.

"They are. Now, do you ladies need anything else?"

"Yes," Elsa-May said. "Some answers. Deena Brown made things for this store, so did you know her well?"

"No. Take the pickled pears 'on the house.'"

Ettie didn't know what the woman meant, so she looked at Elsa-May. "On the house?" Elsa-May repeated, seeming a little perplexed.

"Take them with no payment."

"Are you sure?" Elsa-May said, staring at the jar. Then her eyes widened when she saw the price of twenty-eight dollars.

"Yes. Take them, and please leave. I don't want to hear that woman's name in my store, ever." She walked away from them.

Ettie and Elsa-May stood, staring after her.

"That was odd," Ettie said.

"Oh dear. We probably asked the wrong questions."

"Or, maybe the right ones. Let's go."

When they walked out of the store, they heard someone calling out. "Hey, wait."

They turned around to see a young man with spiky dark hair, and he was wearing an apron.

"Yes?" Elsa-May said.

He pointed to the jar that was in Ettie's hands. "You've got to pay for that."

Ettie saw from the motif on his red apron that he belonged to Amish Dinner. "Mrs. Thripp said it was in the house."

"That's *on* the house, Ettie." Elsa-May explained, "We asked Mrs. Thripp about Deena Brown, who used to make things for the store and she—"

"You shouldn't come here talking about Deena Brown."

Ettie stepped forward. "You knew Deena?"

"Yeah, everyone who works here knew her."

Ettie and Elsa-May looked at one another. "Do you happen to know who owns the store?"

"Mr. Thripp owns it."

"We have heard rumors an Amish woman owns it or is part owner of it."

He shook his head. "I don't know about that." He looked over his shoulder. "I better get back. Sorry to stop you, but she didn't tell me she gave it to you."

"That's fine," Elsa-May said.

"You were only doing your job." Ettie looked back at the store. "I see the sign in the window says you also cater for functions."

"We do. Mrs. Thripp and Sally, her daughter, cater for events. Maybe you can hire them for one of your events. They do large and small. No function is too small."

Elsa-May snorted. "It's unlikely. We have very splendid cooks in our community."

"I'm sure you do." He smiled at them. "Have a lovely day and enjoy your..." he looked at the bottle, "pickled pears."

"We will, and thank you," Elsa-May said. "And it is a sunny day and we will enjoy it."

As they walked down the road, Ettie said, "He was so polite even when he thought we were thieves."

"Did you see what he was wearing?"

"Yes, he was a smart looking man and was well dressed. Immaculate really, so different from the tattered jeans and old faded T shirts many young *Englishers* wear these days. His shoes were also nicely polished."

"I'm talking about what he was wearing around his neck."

"Oh yes, I noticed. A gold chain and it looked like an odd-shaped elongated gold nugget on the end. The end of it was tied to the chain with string."

Elsa-May screwed up her nose. "It's dreadful to see men wearing jewelry. I can understand an *Englisher* woman wearing a chain or a simple ring, but when men do it… it just looks awful. Don't you think?"

Ettie shrugged. "I have no thoughts about it."

"Oh, Ettie. Do you like it, yes or no?"

"I have no opinion about it. I've never given any thought to it."

"Neither have I, but when I saw it just now it looked wrong. Wouldn't you agree?"

Most times, Ettie would simply agree, but sometimes she didn't want to be forced to agree just for the sake of it. Today was one of those times. "I don't care, so I can't say."

"Ettie, why are you always so difficult to get along with?"

"I'm not. Now, let's think about something else."

"Like what?"

Ettie stopped still. "Something about what the young man said."

"Stop stealing and have a nice day? He didn't say much."

"He did, Elsa-May. He said we shouldn't have come there talking about Deena. I think Mrs. Thripp was jealous of Deena and that's why she wanted us to leave. That's why he told us we shouldn't have been there bringing up her name. What if he'd witnessed arguments between Mr. and Mrs. Thripp about Deena?"

"I think you're stretching things a bit far. He didn't say anything of the kind."

"But did you see how Mrs. Thripp acted when Deena was mentioned?"

"That's true. Do you think she killed Deena because she thought her husband was straying?" Elsa-May asked.

"Possibly." Ettie looked at the jar in her hands. "I wonder if Deena made this?"

"There's every chance. Mrs. Thripp said she can't keep them on the shelf and Mr. Thripp used to collect jars of food from Deena two or three times a week."

"These pickled pears could have been one of their better sellers. And, something else I noticed."

"What's that?"

"You said they don't make food and they do. They are caterers and that means they do make meals for people." Ettie was delighted her sister was wrong.

"Ach, you're stretching things again. I said they're not a diner, and they're not. Let's just go home. I'm weary."

Ettie smiled as she clutched her jar of pickled pears. "Okay. I think we've done all we can for one day." Ettie looked down at her jar and for the first time noticed the price. "Oh, Elsa-May did you see the price of these pears?"

"I did. And it surprises me that you'd think of buying such a high-priced item. We could buy several boxes of fresh pears for that money and make our own."

"I didn't look at the price until just now."

Elsa-May stuck her nose in the air. "That means you have more money than sense."

Ettie turned around to face the Amish Dinner store. "I'll take them back."

Elsa-May grabbed the jar out of Ettie's hands. "We're not going back there after you made such a scene. Come along." Elsa-May walked off and Ettie hurried to catch up.

CHAPTER 21

That night, Detective Kelly knocked on Elsa-May and Ettie's door.

Ettie opened the door for him and hoped he had welcome news. "Come in." Ettie accidently stepped back onto Elsa-May's foot causing her to yelp. "I'm sorry, I didn't see you there, Elsa-May."

Elsa-May's face contorted with pain. "You always do that!"

"If that's true, you should keep out of my way."

"You know I have sore feet."

Kelly drew his eyebrows together. "Are you all right, Mrs. Lutz?"

"I will be when the pain ceases."

"Let me help you to your chair." Ettie put her arm around Elsa-May's waist and walked her over.

When Elsa-May was seated, she looked up at Kelly.

"I've had sore feet all day. I was wearing new shoes and Ettie still had me doing a lot of walking."

Kelly sat down on a chair opposite the couch where Ettie usually sat. "I see there's a for sale sign on the house next door."

"There is?" Ettie asked.

"It must've gone up after we got home, Ettie. I wonder why Gabriel didn't—"

"Someone else must've put it up," Ettie suggested.

"*Jah,* must've. Maybe."

"Gabriel Yoder is selling the house next door and he wants us to show the buyers through," Ettie told Detective Kelly.

"Good luck with that. I hope he gets some takers."

"It was for sale for a very long time before he bought it. I think it was an impulse buy that he later regretted."

"Humph. Must have more money than sense," Detective Kelly said, "considering what happened there."

His comment reminded Ettie of the pickled pear incident with her sister earlier that day.

"It's quite possible," Elsa-May said.

"You know that you have to disclose to all the potential buyers that there was a murder there, don't you?"

The sisters looked at each other.

"We'll tell them if they're seriously interested,"

Elsa-May answered. "Otherwise there's no point talking about it."

"Okay. Suit yourselves. Where did you go today to make your feet so sore, Mrs. Lutz?"

Ettie clasped her hands in her lap. "We went here and there, everywhere really. I hope you're here to tell us that you've released poor Annie."

"I did. I held her as long as I could, and eventually—."

"Ah, at last. I'm so pleased," Ettie said.

"Me too. No more cat trays. Would you like a cup of hot tea, Detective?" Elsa-May asked.

"I won't thanks. I'm on my way home and the wife is keeping my meal warm. One night my missus and I might get to sit down together to eat."

"Oh, that must be awful. It's hardly a nice life for you."

"I'm committed, Mrs. Lutz. Committed to giving people answers when their loved ones are murdered. The families deserve closure. There's no greater satisfaction than what I feel when I see the looks on their faces when the killer is convicted. That's what keeps me doing my job each day. It's a calling."

"It must be." Ettie clasped her hands together in her lap. "Have there been any other developments?"

"That's why I'm here. The first forty-eight hours in an investigation like this are the most crucial, as you've probably heard me say once or twice over the years.

Sadly, we're past that point now. We're now in day four. I'm hoping that you two have learned something."

Ettie looked over at Elsa-May, who nodded, giving her permission to tell him. She looked back at Kelly and took a deep breath. "It seems that Deena was escaping from someone. Someone who wanted to do her harm."

He nodded. "Mrs. Lapp told me that, eventually. We ran his name through the system—Enrico Garcia—and found out he's in jail. Has been for over ten years. Manslaughter, that's the official charge."

"Oh. Annie knew his name?"

"Yes, but apparently, not the part about him being in jail."

"He could've got someone else to kill Deena," Elsa-May said.

"I thought of that, but why now?" Detective Kelly asked.

Ettie couldn't even look at Elsa-May right now. That had been exactly what she'd said.

Kelly crossed one leg over the other. "Annie claims she's innocent. Deena's estranged son has suddenly gone missing, and Deena's only enemy, that we know of, is incarcerated." He shook his head. "There were no signs on the road that someone accidently ran her down and, besides that, the injuries weren't consistent with that scenario. I can tell you that's what my first thought was with her being so close to the road like she was."

"I wonder if the son is running for his life. If that

Enrico Garcia fellow sent someone to kill her, Ryker might be next on the list. That's why Annie told him to run."

"But why, Ettie?"

"I don't know."

Kelly rubbed his chin. "I wasn't going to say, but you should probably know some things for you to move forward with your questioning."

"What is it?" Ettie asked.

"The man in jail is Ryker's father."

Ettie and Elsa-May looked at each other in shock.

Kelly continued, "Even though he's a career criminal, it's unlikely he would've killed Deena. She was his bookkeeper, and when his wife was killed in a drive-by shooting, he asked Deena to take the boy and hide him."

"Just like Moses," Elsa-May said.

Kelly shook his head. "I don't think so. Anyway, he had an arrangement whereby he sent Deena money. We checked that out and it's true. He sent Deena money until the boy was eighteen."

"I never saw that coming," Ettie said.

"I meant Moses was hidden, that's all," Elsa-May let the detective know.

Kelly raised his eyebrows and then went on, "We're heading to a dead end. I don't like this. Normally there are more suspects, more leads, more clues." Kelly shook his head. "I don't mind telling you this one's got me baffled. I've got everyone working on it. We've got a board of visuals to help us piece together a timeline. We need to know Deena's movements in her last days —who she talked to, where she went."

"We'll help," said Elsa-May.

He rubbed his chin. "Thank you. I know when I've tried to get information out of you Amish people before, many of you have a habit of not answering your doors."

Ettie knew that's why he was there. He needed their help to form the timeline. "We'll keep talking to people and see what we can find out."

"Would you?"

"Yes. We'll do it," Ettie said.

"I appreciate it. Normally, we can do that without moving from the computer. There'd be bank transactions, phone records, things like that, and they would pinpoint her location, but because she's Amish we've got none of that. That's why I'm relying on the both of you to flesh out those details."

"The note!"

Kelly looked at Ettie. "What?"

"You took the note that Deena wrote. What happened with that?"

"It's being examined right now. We still don't have a full report on the crime scene either. These things take a while to come back to us."

"Annie's home now?"

"I don't know where she went after she left the station. She left accompanied by your bishop."

"He would've taken her home," Ettie said. "She wouldn't have let her cats stay another night by themselves."

Kelly frowned at the mention of cats. Then he rubbed his arms. "I'm sure the both of you will turn up something."

"We'll try, won't we, Elsa-May?"

"We will. As long as… are you sure Enrico Garcia wouldn't have paid someone to harm Deena for some reason?"

"Your friend Annie, was wrong about him. Now, I don't know if she deliberately told lies or whether she was told lies by Deena. Annie is under the impression Garcia's a jilted lover from years ago. I have arranged to talk with him tomorrow. I won't leave any lead unfollowed or any stone unturned until I find who killed Deena Brown." He rubbed his ribs.

"Are you sure you wouldn't like a cup of hot tea?" Ettie asked.

Elsa-May moved to the edge of her chair. "We might even have a piece of cake left over."

"No, thank you."

"The cake's fresh," Ettie told him. "It's not left over at all. The bishop's wife baked it and everyone loves her cakes."

He raised his hands. "I'll have to pass." He rose to his feet. "The wife will be wondering where I am. She expected me home half an hour ago."

Ettie walked Detective Kelly to the door, stood there

and waited for him to get in his car. Once he drove away, she closed the door and headed to let Snowy out of Elsa-May's bedroom. As usual, Snowy scampered around sniffing everywhere Detective Kelly had been.

"Ettie, why did you say the cake was fresh? Of course it would be, we wouldn't give him stale cake."

Ettie sat back on her couch. "I know, but from what you said, it sounded like you wanted to give him left-over cake. In my head, I pictured one lonely piece left in a tin at the back of the pantry."

Elsa-May chuckled. "You do have an imagination."

"Not really. He turned it down. When was the last time he turned down cake or cookies? Or any kind of food? He must have shared that image of the moldy cake."

"I don't think so. It's in your mind and your mind alone. And, he has turned down our food since he's been married. Now he has someone waiting for him at home, and he's changed."

"For the better."

"That's right. I'm happy for him. He was lonely before."

"That was certainly a shock. Ryker's father is a criminal and his mother was killed. That's very sad. It was kind of Deena to look after Ryker like she did."

"Ettie, why didn't you tell the detective about Mrs. Thripp?"

"Why didn't you? I was waiting for you to mention it. Why is everything always up to me?"

"It's not."

"Then why didn't you tell him?" Ettie asked.

Elsa-May sighed. "Forget it. I can see you don't really think Mrs. Thripp killed Deena, or you would've told him."

"I wouldn't say that."

"You wouldn't say that, like you wouldn't inform Kelly." Elsa-May held up her hand. "I don't want to talk about murders or suspects or anything like that tonight."

"Fine."

Snowy stopped sniffing around, headed to his dog bed in the corner of the room and made himself comfortable, placing his head between his paws.

Ettie smiled admiring Snowy's dark eyes and nose peeping out of his woolly white fur. Then her mind drifted to Deena. "I've been thinking, Elsa-May. I'm sure Annie wrote that note that was supposedly from Deena."

Through gritted teeth, Elsa-May said, "You're talking about something you're not supposed to talk about."

"Sorry."

A minute later, Elsa-May said, "Why would Annie have written it?"

Ettie shrugged. "That's the question."

"What's the answer? If there's a question there must be an answer."

Ettie narrowed her eyes at her sister. Was she trying

to be argumentative or did it just come naturally? "That's what we have to figure out."

Elsa-May reached down into the bag by her feet and pulled out her knitting. "There's another approach we could take."

"What is it?"

"We'll ask Annie if she wrote it, and if she says yes, we'll ask why."

Ettie stared at her sister. Sometimes she had good ideas.

CHAPTER 22

The next day, Ettie and Elsa-May found Annie at home. She ushered them into the kitchen and they sat at the table.

"It was horrible, sitting in that jail cell. I never did anything wrong. He kept asking me questions."

"Who did?" Elsa-May asked.

"Detective Kelly, mostly. Then a younger man came in and had a turn asking. I gave them the same answers. I don't know anything about anything. I can't remember the last time I saw Deena and that's what I told them."

Ettie looked at Elsa-May, who gave her a nod. "Annie, I'm going to ask you something and I need you to tell me the truth."

Her eyes opened wide. "I'd never tell you anything else."

"That note that Detective Kelly took..."

Elsa-May jumped in, "Was it from Deena, or did you write it? Because it looks like your hand-writing. *Jah,* that's right. Ettie found something you'd written and she said it looked the same as the writing on the note that you said was from Deena."

Ettie was surprised at her sister. The gentle approach would've been better. Why was Elsa-May so confrontational all the time?

Annie looked at both of them in turn, then she hung her head. "I wrote it."

Ettie was surprised—her sister's blunt approach had worked. "Why?"

"Does the detective know?" Elsa-May asked.

Annie shook her head. "He doesn't. I suppose I'll have to tell you everything now, won't I?"

"Most definitely," Ettie said.

"Deena came to me days ago and told me that she had to go into hiding, but she wanted me to help her make everyone believe she was still at her home."

"Into hiding?" Elsa-May asked.

"Why?"

"She told me all about that dreadful man she was running from. She told me that if anything ever happened to her, to tell Ryker to run. She gave me all his phone numbers a while back, his cell phone and his work number, and she kept giving me his new ones over the years. It took me a few hours to remember to call him because I was in such shock. As soon as I remembered, I called him." Annie sighed. "That's what happened. He found her and killed her. I'm sure of it."

Ettie was silent for a moment while she processed Annie's words.

"Going back to the note, that doesn't make any sense at all. If she was hiding from someone, why would she make believe she was still here, sick at home?" Elsa-May asked. "Wouldn't it be better for the person who was after her to think she'd gone somewhere?"

"That's something I can't tell you."

Elsa-May leaned forward, her bottom jaw sticking out. "You just said you'd tell us everything. I don't think you are."

Ettie patted her sister's shoulder, hoping she'd calm down. There was no reason for anyone to get upset.

"I'm not keeping anything from you. I can't tell you, Elsa-May, because I don't know."

"Well, what do you know?" Elsa-May shot back.

Annie swallowed hard. "My mouth's dry."

Ettie pushed herself to her feet. "I'll get you a glass of water."

"*Denke,* Ettie."

While Ettie filled the glass, she said, "We're only trying to find out who killed Deena. What if he kills again?" Annie didn't answer. Ettie put the water in front of her and sat down again.

After Annie took a sip, she said, "The ladies want to come here for a meeting. They're worried that the killer might strike again. They want to discuss what precautions we should take. I can't tell them about the man who was after Deena, because no one would like it that I kept that to myself. Besides, the police haven't caught him yet."

Elsa-May frowned. "What do you know that we don't know, Annie?"

Ettie had to wonder why Annie was telling that story about the man from Deena's past. Was she lying or is that what Deena had told her?

"Deena came here, and I can't even tell you what day it was, but she said she wanted to get away. She wasn't safe, and those were her very words."

Ettie moved uncomfortably in the hard-wooden chair. "Wasn't safe from what, or from whom? Did she give you a name?"

"She didn't have to. I knew about her past. He was coming to take his revenge by killing her. She was always afraid he'd find her one day. She talked about it all the time."

Ettie tried to piece everything together with what Detective Kelly had told them. "You think this man from her past killed her?"

"Yes."

"Then why didn't you tell the police that?"

"I did. I told them. They thought I knew something else, but I didn't. Just like the both of you."

"Why write the fake note?"

Annie stared at Elsa-May. "I told you. She wanted

everyone to think she was still around. I wanted the quilting bee ladies to think she wasn't coming and she'd said so. They know she's always involved in every sewing event. Next meeting that came around, I was to tell the bishop and Mary that she was ill and that I was caring for her. That way, she wouldn't get visitors."

Elsa-May shook her head. "This gets us no closer to finding out who killed her."

"I just told you. It must've been that man—the man from her past."

"*Jah*, but no one saw him, did they?"

Ettie was pleased Elsa-May also didn't let Annie know that the man in question was in prison. Detective Kelly must've kept that from her for a reason.

"No, but there was no one else who could've done it," Annie said.

Ettie remembered they had to piece together Deena's last few days for Detective Kelly. "Tell me about the last few times you saw her."

"Let's see now. When she told me she was going, when she was here. The time before that, is when we went to the markets together. It was a week before that. And then the time before that, would've been at the Sunday meeting."

"Did she seem okay, or was she acting differently?" Elsa-May asked.

"*Nee*. She was being normal. Didn't seem worried or anything. When she came to my house was the only time she seemed upset out of all the time I've known her. We were friends because I lived the closest to her out of anyone in the community."

"That makes sense, I suppose," Elsa-May said.

One of the cats jumped on the table. "Pepper, get down!"

The cat gave a yowl, jumped off the table and ran out of the room.

"Oh, I do feel awful for speaking harshly to him just now," Annie said.

"I'm sure the cat will get over it."

Annie scowled at Elsa-May. "They're not like dogs. They have feelings."

Ettie said to Annie, "So, as far as you know, Deena ran away because she learned that this man from her past found out where she was?"

"That's correct."

"How did she know that he found out where she was?" Ettie asked.

Annie shook her head. "She didn't say."

"Someone had to have told her," Elsa-May said.

"They must've, but I don't know who. The police tell me Ryker is missing. I hope that man didn't kill him, too."

Elsa-May added, "I hope not, but since you told him to run, it makes sense that he's missing."

"Annie, it would help if you knew what she did or who she spoke to in her last few days."

"I can't help you with that, Ettie. Nothing seemed out of the ordinary. I agreed to all her demands about pretending she had never gone anywhere. I felt I had to. I never knew what would've happened."

"And that was a few days before she died?" Elsa-May asked.

"A few days before she was found," Annie said.

"That means it might have been the day Deena died, or close to it."

Ettie frowned at Elsa-May, when Annie hung her head. She'd just made Annie feel worse.

"I failed her," Annie whimpered.

Ettie leaned over and patted Annie's arm. "You did the best you could and that's all any of us can ever do."

"Tell that to the police. They think I'm not telling them the truth. They probably think I did it, but I didn't."

"Of course you didn't," Ettie said.

"*Nee.* I don't think you did," Elsa-May added. "But did you tell them all that you told us?"

"I can't recall. Everything is fuzzy. I've never been in jail before."

"You should tell them that you wrote that note and tell them why. It won't hurt and it could help. You'll be worse off if they find out for themselves and you were keeping it from them. You don't want to get arrested for impeding an investigation or withholding information."

"Can I get arrested for that?"

"I think so," Elsa-May said.

Annie nodded. "I will tell the detective if you think it's best."

"I do, and they'll find out soon anyway, so best you tell them beforehand." Ettie looked up at the ceiling. "I would love it if there was some way that we could find out where she went and who she talked with."

"Come here tomorrow and find out from the ladies. They're all coming here at twelve for a luncheon to talk about what's happened."

"Who's coming?" Elsa-May asked.

"All my friends. The sewing ladies. Deena was one of them. Someone might have seen her somewhere or talked with her."

Elsa-May looked over at Ettie, who nodded. "All right, we'll be here," Elsa-May said. "What time did you say?"

"She said twelve." Ettie stared at Annie and hoped that she was telling the truth as she knew it. She had a feeling she wasn't, and she didn't know how to get any more information out of her.

"Can I ask you both something?" Annie asked.

"Sure," Ettie said.

"If you see the detective can you tell him for me?"

"About the note?" Elsa-May asked.

Annie nodded.

"We can, but he'll want to hear it from you."

"Then I will confirm it."

"Okay, we'll tell him." Ettie sighed. She wasn't looking forward to it.

"When is Luke due back?"

"Any day now, I hope. I'll feel better about this whole thing once he's here."

On the way home that day, Ettie called Detective Kelly to tell him about the note.

"Is that you, Mrs. Smith?"

"Yes."

"I can barely hear you. It's a bad connection. I'm at the correctional center about to talk to Enrico Garcia. I'll see you both tomorrow." He ended the call.

Ettie replaced the receiver.

"What did he say, Ettie?"

"He said he's about to talk to Enrico Garcia and he'd talk to us tomorrow." Ettie sighed. "I don't know if that means he's coming to see us or if we're supposed to visit him."

"You didn't tell him that Annie wrote that note?"

"I didn't have the chance." Ettie sighed again. "It's bad she hasn't told him before now. You would think that when she was being held in jail, she would've told him everything."

"Come on, let's go. Snowy's waiting for us. It'll all work itself out."

"I hope so."

Arm-in-arm, the elderly sisters walked home.

CHAPTER 23

The next day, all the ladies were gathered in Annie's house to talk about the killer on the loose.

Maggie Overberg was the first to talk. "I'm so worried that I can't sleep. Since someone has been killed, the murderer might target us ladies and kill us off one at a time. What do you think, Ettie?"

Ettie shrugged her shoulders. "There's no evidence to suggest that." As soon as she said it, she recognized it as something Kelly would say.

"I'm not going to sit around and wait for evidence. We need to do something now." Maggie's voice rose.

"Like what?" Mary, the bishop's wife, asked.

"We'll not go outdoors at all. Not by ourselves. We'll travel in groups. *Jah,* that's a great idea. Mary, you'll have to suggest that to Paul."

"Do you think so?" Mary asked.

"It might be the only thing that keeps us safe. They hit Deena over the head with a rock, but next time they might use a gun. They'll gun us down and we won't see it coming."

"Everyone, calm down. One woman was killed. It doesn't mean that anyone else will be," Elsa-May said.

"Jah, but you don't know that for certain do you?" one of the ladies asked.

"Of course I can't be certain, but let's not panic."

"We want to prepare ourselves just in case. We need to be careful or do you object to that too, Elsa-May?"

Elsa-May shook her head, then Ettie and Elsa-May exchanged glances. Each knew what the other was thinking. It was no use talking at all. The other ladies weren't listening to a word.

Katie, one of the younger women, said, "Does anyone else think it's funny that Deena's husband just disappeared? After all these years no one has seen or heard from him."

"What are you saying about that?" Annie asked.

"Well, what if he's dead? I always wondered if she killed him. Now someone's killed her. An eye-for-an-eye."

"Don't be ridiculous," Annie said. "Nothing like that ever happened. If anyone says anything like that in my *haus* again I will ask them to leave."

Katie hung her head. "I'm sorry, Annie."

"He's probably gone somewhere and he'll be back

one day. Does everyone know Deena's funeral is tomorrow?" Mary asked everyone.

"Already?" Annie asked.

"That was quick," Julia, another of the younger ladies, said.

"Yes. Everyone is to be at my *haus* at ten in the morning."

"We'll be there." Ettie knew she would have to tell the detective that the funeral was tomorrow. She wanted to deliver the news in person rather than tell him by phone.

"I've got a bad feeling about this," Maggie said. "I think there'll be more murders. This is the first of many, mark my words."

Ettie had to stop herself from rolling her eyes. Maggie was either gossiping about things or having bad feelings about everything.

"I don't think we have to worry. I don't think we're all going to be murdered in our beds," Elsa-May said.

"We are just trying to prevent a problem before it becomes a problem. What do you think, Annie?" Maggie asked.

"I know everybody's worried in case it happens again. Do you think we should take precautions? I'm been thinking that people shouldn't go out alone or go for any walks by themselves like she must have done. It's just not worth the risk," Annie said.

"I agree," Maggie blurted out.

"There's nothing wrong with taking precautions. I

don't want anyone worrying unnecessarily." Elsa-May's gaze ran over the group of around fifteen women, crammed into Annie's living room.

"It's better than being murdered like dear old Deena was," one of the ladies said.

"She wasn't that old, was she?" Ettie asked. "She was only young, I mean, she wasn't that old. She was somewhere in her forties, I'm guessing."

"That's old to me," Julia said.

"And how old are you, Julia?"

"Twenty-two."

"I heard someone say it had something to do with her past. Has she brought dangerous people to the community?" Katie suggested.

"Where did you hear that?" Ettie asked.

Katie glanced at Maggie, and then said, "I don't know, it was just something I overheard."

"I heard some rumors about her and a man who owned a store in town," Katie said.

Maggie said, "No one believes that."

"I'm just saying that I heard about it."

"Don't spread rumors." Maggie shook a finger at her.

Ettie found it odd that Maggie was the one doing the reprimanding. Now she knew that it was true about the rumors between Deena and Mr. Thripp if the word had reached those in the community. It wasn't just Wayne who was concerned.

"Did anyone see Deena, outside of the Sunday meetings, in the last couple of weeks?" Elsa-May asked.

Everyone shook their heads and a few murmured 'no.' Then the conversation turned back to the killer, who might be next to die, and what they could do about it.

Ettie couldn't wait to get out of the room and she saw the same exasperation written over Elsa-May's face as well.

It was one of these meetings where everyone wanted a chance to have their say, no decisions would be made, they would go around in circles for hours, and they would never get to the point.

Right at that moment, a fly fell into Ettie's tea and she bounded to her feet.

"What is it, Ettie?"

"There's a fly in my tea. It's not in there now. It must've taken a quick dip and it flew out again."

Maggie giggled. "Don't worry, Ettie," she said. "I'm sure it didn't drink much."

Annie stood up, gave Maggie a reproving look, and reached for Ettie's cup. "Oh Ettie, I'm so sorry. Let me fix you another one."

Ettie screwed up her nose. "It's fine. I'll do it." Ettie moved to the kitchen and threw the remainder of her tea down the sink, rinsed out the cup, and poured herself another one. She'd only just set the teapot down on the table when Elsa-May joined her.

"Are you ready to go?" Elsa-May whispered.

"I was ready to go as soon as I got here."

Elsa-May chuckled. "How long do you think we'll have to be here?"

"I think we have to stay until I finish this cup."

"I agree. When you're ready to leave, just say the word."

"I will. And then we will have to do something useful. Because this is a complete waste of time. No one knows anything. No one saw her and no one heard from her in those last days. You know what Detective Kelly said about the clock ticking?"

"I know."

They walked back out to the living room and sat down.

CHAPTER 24

When Ettie and Elsa-May were home, they wondered how they'd get to the funeral the next day. No one had offered to pick them up.

"Jeremiah and Ava normally take us to funerals. They haven't stopped by to arrange anything."

"Maybe they did and we were out."

Just then there was a knock at the door. Elsa-May's face lit up. "That might be Jeremiah now."

Ettie was first to the door to open it. It was their friend Gabriel.

"Come in," Ettie said. "I thought you left."

"I'm waiting for the funeral, like I said."

"Someone looked through the house already. We thought you must've left."

"Oh, they must've seen it for sale on one of the

flyers I placed in the stores. I'm sorry to have you do the showings."

"That's okay."

"What did they think of it?" he asked. "Do they want to buy it?"

The sisters looked at one another.

"I'm not sure. They're thinking about it." Ettie asked, "Do you remember Ryker Lapp?"

"You already asked me already, Ettie. I said I do. I suspect we'll see him at the funeral tomorrow."

Elsa-May frowned. "Maybe. When you told us the other day you saw her on a road with the buggy wheel in a ditch, where was she exactly?"

"Just on a stretch of road out toward the old deserted mill."

"Could you take us there?" Ettie asked.

"I can drive you there after the funeral perhaps. Would you like me to take you to the funeral? And after that I'll have to pack for my trip."

"Thank you, Gabriel. We'd like that," Ettie told him.

CHAPTER 25

Before Gabriel picked them up on the day of Deena's funeral, Ettie decided to take Snowy for a quick walk and, at the same time, call Detective Kelly to let him know the funeral would take place that morning.

"Thank you, Mrs. Smith. Your bishop already informed me. I'll try to make it to the graveyard."

"What happened with Enrico Garcia? Did you get to talk with him?"

"He said he's not angry at Deena or at anyone; it's ancient history. He's done a lot of thinking, a lot of work on himself, and he claims to be rehabilitated. He told me what I already knew about him and he seemed genuine."

"Do you believe him?"

"Yes. He's not our killer, and by that, I mean I don't think he would've arranged for someone to kill Deena either. He claims to not even know of her whereabouts these last few years. I asked him about his son. He paid Deena, who was once his bookkeeper, to look after his child because he was always in trouble with the law. I had the impression he paid her for more than that, cooking the books they call it, but I'm not investigating that side of things."

"Did you tell Enrico Garcia what happened to Deena?"

"Yes, that's why I was there."

"I wasn't sure."

"He didn't show any emotion but, as I said, I still don't think he's our man. I have to go now, Mrs. Smith. I've got a full day."

"Very well." Before she could say goodbye, he'd already ended the call. She hung up the phone's receiver then she looked down at Snowy. "Some people don't even say goodbye. Let's go home and see if your *Mamm* is finished getting dressed."

AT THE VIEWING in the bishop's house prior to the funeral, Ettie was surprised to see Ryker, but he wasn't the only surprise. Luke, Annie's husband, had returned from Ohio. Ryker was the only *Englisher* in attendance and even though he wore a dark suit, he stood out because his hair was cropped short. She wondered if she should call Detective Kelly, but seeing it was a funeral, it didn't seem appropriate.

She approached him. "Hello, Ryker. I wasn't sure you'd be here today."

The young man turned around. He lowered his head. "Mrs. Smith, isn't it?"

"It is."

"I thought you were dead."

Ettie couldn't believe her ears. "What do you mean?"

"I'm sorry. I thought you died years ago."

"I'm still here. I'm sorry about your mother." Her first impression was that he wasn't polite.

"Thank you."

"I'm sorry you didn't get along with her."

He stared at her, narrowing his dark brown eyes. "It wasn't easy, so I didn't try."

"Do you know who might have killed her?"

He raised his eyebrows, looked around, and shoved his hands into the pockets of his pants. "I don't."

"Are you hiding from someone?" Ettie asked.

"What?"

"You got that call from Annie to run, and then you disappeared. I thought you might be hiding and that's why."

He huffed and looked around again. "Why so many questions? This is a funeral."

Ettie stepped closer. "Because of that very reason. It

is a funeral and I'm trying to find out who killed Deena."

"Why, to thank them?"

It was a dreadful thing to say, and there was no hint of amusement on his face, so he hadn't said it to be funny. "Why do you say things like that about your mother?"

"Firstly, she wasn't my mother; she only kept me for the money."

"What money?"

"Money my father had to keep sending her. He was always in and out of trouble, in and out of prison. He couldn't help himself. He came for me once and she wouldn't let me go. I heard them arguing. She was holding something over his head." He pressed his lips together.

"What was it?"

He shook his head. "I've no idea."

"Did you ask him?"

"No. I don't know him. He was never around. I've never talked to him and I only ever saw him that day."

"But he's your father."

"Only by name. Hezekiah was the man who was my real father, but something happened to him."

"What do you think happened?"

"It doesn't matter now. What's done is done. If you want to know about Deena, just know that all she was after was money."

"She had everything she could want here in the community. Why would she need or want money?"

"I can't answer that one, Mrs. Smith. I'm not a psychiatrist. Now that she's dead, I'm free. Free to be the person I should've been at the start."

Ettie shook her head. "I can't believe what I'm hearing. She raised you when your father couldn't."

"That's your opinion. You want to know the truth about her?"

"Yes."

"Come here." He strode out of the house and Ettie followed. Once they were clear of the house, he turned to face her. "Deena killed Hezekiah."

"Killed him? He disappeared. No one ever said he was dead."

"I know it. She flew into terrible rages. One morning, he said he didn't like his eggs runny, the next thing I know she hits him over the head with a frypan in front of me. He was knocked to the floor, and he was dead."

Ettie couldn't believe it was true. "But he's not dead, he disappeared."

"That's the story she told everyone. After it happened, she yelled at me to get to my room. I went to my room and I was allowed out for supper that night. She told me they had an argument and he left." He shook his head. "She knew I saw him lying on the floor."

"Why didn't you report it?"

"I was only twelve at the time. Who were they going to believe? I've no idea what she did with the body. But when they find it, they'll find his skull was crushed. It had to have been."

Ettie hung her head.

"Err, I'm sorry, Mrs. Smith. It sounds like you had no idea the type of woman she was."

Ettie shook her head. "I always thought of her as a lovely woman who liked sewing."

"She wasn't. The reason I'm here is to celebrate, not commiserate." He went to walk away and then turned around. "If you don't believe me about my stepfather, have them dig around the house. A skinny woman like her wouldn't have had the strength to drag his body too far."

"Where can I find you if I need to talk with you again?"

"I don't want to talk anymore."

Ettie walked closer. "Please talk to the police. It makes you look guilty if you disappear completely. There is a detective in town named Detective Kelly. He has to hear what you've got to say."

"Why would I worry about looking guilty?"

"Because you were close to Deena and the police always investigate those closest. If you disappear, they'll think you're guilty."

"You tell him what happened."

Shaking her head, Ettie said, "He'll never listen to me. He won't look for a body unless he has strong evidence, or if someone like you says what you know."

"Like I said, it won't bring him back, and I don't want to hang around for an investigation."

He went to walk away again, but Ettie grabbed his sleeve and he turned around. "How do I know what you say is true? Maybe you killed Deena."

He grinned. "It wasn't me, but I knew it would happen one day."

"Why do you say that?"

"I believe in karma. An eye for an eye and all that. She took a life and someone took hers."

Ettie tried her best to sum up the young man. "Does anyone else know she killed Hezekiah?"

"Maybe. I wouldn't know. I'll see you around some-time, Mrs. Smith."

This time, he walked away and Ettie knew she shouldn't ask more questions.

"Ettie."

Elsa-May passed Ryker and continued on to Ettie. "What did he say to you?"

"You'll never believe me."

"Try me."

Ettie held her hand up, and whispered, "Come sit in the buggy."

Once they were sitting in Gabriel's buggy, Elsa-May took a couple of deep breaths.

"Are you okay?"

"I think I am. I should have had breakfast."

"*Jah,* well that's what happens when you sleep in and we have someone picking us up."

"I know. What did Ryker tell you?"

"You will never believe it."

"You said that already. Nothing would surprise me. Does he know who killed her?"

"No, but he did tell me that Deena killed Hezekiah."

Elsa-May's jaw fell open. "No!"

"Yes. According to him, she hit him over the head with a frying pan when he said that he didn't like runny eggs."

Slowly, Elsa-May nodded.

"Aren't you shocked?" Ettie asked.

"I am, but it can be annoying when people complain about your food after you've taken a long time to cook it."

"But not quite annoying enough to kill somebody over it. Maybe he's lying."

Elsa-May shook her head. "I don't think he would have any reason to do that."

"So you believe him?" Ettie asked.

"I think I do."

"Why? He ran away years ago, so he's probably trying to muddy Deena's name to make himself feel better."

"I don't think so. Why don't you believe him?"

Ettie sighed. "I didn't say I didn't. I tried to get him to talk with Detective Kelly, but he wouldn't."

"No one would talk to him if they didn't have to."

"Now Kelly is never going to look for a body without hearing directly from an eyewitness. The story has always been that Hezekiah disappeared. Yes, it was out of character, but Kelly would say it's not the first time it's happened."

"He would say that. He says that about everything. I can hear him now."

Ettie bit her lip. "I just can't see her doing it. Now I think about it more, it seems preposterous."

"I know, but we didn't know the woman very well. Were those her secrets, Ettie? She killed Hezekiah, and Ryker wasn't her son?"

"And, the other secret could be she was hiding from the man in jail and she thought he wanted to kill her. According to Kelly, he hadn't given her a thought for years. I guess that's true because Ryker's all grown up now."

"Go talk to Ryker some more, Ettie. He must know more about Deena."

"I can't leave you."

"I'll be fine. I just need some food."

Ettie spied a box of fruit in the back of Gabriel's buggy. She reached over the back and picked out a mandarin. "Here. Have this."

"*Denke.* I'll eat this, you talk to him before he leaves. He might not be coming to the gravesite."

Ettie took a deep breath, hoping he'd talk to her. "Okay." She hurried back to Ryker, who was now talking to the bishop. She stood behind him, waiting politely until they finished speaking.

"Excuse me," Ettie said as soon as Ryker turned around.

"Oh, it's you again."

"Yes, and I'm still alive."

He grinned.

"You said Deena wasn't your real mother, so do you know what happened to your birthmother?"

"She's dead, and my father has spent most of his life sitting in jail."

"One thing I can't work out is why you were told to run."

"Oh, that message from Annie Lapp. I honestly don't know. The woman must be mad. I got the message and it made no sense to me."

"So, why did you disappear when you got it?"

He scratched the back of his neck. "Why all the questions, Mrs. Smith?"

"I'm trying to figure out who killed Deena."

"Do you think my answers will help you in any way?"

"Yes."

"Enrico Garcia was paying her to look after me, I found out. She told me she stole me, and half a dozen weird and wonderful stories over the years. I think she was blackmailing my father as well."

"I think he might have been sending her money to look after you, provide for you."

He sighed. "Obviously, he was sending some for that. I wasn't told the details."

"But you just said..."

"Yes, she was getting money out of him," he snapped.

"It wouldn't have been a lot, would it? I think the detective in charge of the case confirmed she was getting money to support you, but I don't think it was in the amount that a blackmailer would receive."

He frowned. "I'm not sure. Excuse me." He took a large stride to one side and went to walk away and was confronted by Maggie and Mary.

Ettie walked back to Elsa-May but before she got there, Luke caught up with her. "Ettie, I want to thank you for looking after Annie when I wasn't here. She said you fed the cats."

"I did. Along with Elsa-May."

"I'm very grateful."

"You're very welcome. It was nothing really, no effort. We enjoyed doing it. It must've been hard for you when Hezekiah disappeared."

He nodded. "It was and Deena dying so suddenly has brought it all back. I mean, there's his property just sitting there. I don't even know if he's alive or dead."

"Have you heard any rumors about what might have happened to him?"

"In this community, there is always talk. Everyone just wants to help."

"Have you heard any rumors regarding Deena and your brother's disappearance?"

He drew his greying eyebrows together. "What rumors?"

Ettie knew she was treading on dangerous ground. "Oh, nothing. I must go to Elsa-May, she's not feeling well."

He smiled at her, gave her a nod and she headed to Elsa-May.

Once she was seated in the buggy, everyone came out of the bishop's house following the coffin.

The sisters watched the coffin as it was loaded onto the specially made buggy, and then Gabriel got into the front seat.

Ettie had to wait until they were at the graveyard before she told her sister more. She didn't want Gabriel to overhear.

One by one, the long trail of buggies wove in and out of the streets until they arrived at the graveyard that was shared by the Mennonites and the Amish.

Gabriel stopped the buggy. "How are you feeling now, Elsa-May?"

"Still a little weak."

"I'll stay with her," Ettie said.

"I can take you both home now if you like. You don't have to wait. Everyone will understand."

"We'll be fine. I'd like to sit and watch," Elsa-May said.

"Okay."

Once he walked away, Elsa-May asked what Ettie had found out.

"Ah, now this is interesting. The man who is in jail, Enrico Garcia, wasn't some crazed ex-lover trying to kill Deena like we first thought. He was paying her to look after his son while he was in prison. What if she knew about some other crime he'd committed and she threatened to expose him?"

"Oh, Ettie. That sounds ridiculous. What would she want with money? She lived in a modest home in the Amish community. We don't have the use for a lot of money."

"Maybe the reason she needed it was because of another secret. We should find out if she had any money in the bank. Kelly would've said if she had a great deal, but what if she had another account at a different bank?"

"*Jah,* it's possible. Ill-gotten gains—filthy lucre."

"We'll soon find out, if we can get Kelly to agree to it."

They looked out the window of the buggy. Everyone had gathered around the grave and the men were now lowering the coffin to the ground.

"I'm not so sad now, after finding out she's a murderer," Elsa-May said.

"Allegedly," Ettie said. "You can't believe one person."

"You don't think Ryker's a reliable witness?"

"I don't know. It's his word against hers, and she's

dead." Ettie trembled. She didn't want to think ill of the woman, but Ryker had cast doubts into her mind.

"Let's have Gabriel take us into town and from there we will talk to Kelly."

"*Nee.* I think you should go home."

"I'm fine after that piece of fruit."

Ettie leaned over the back and passed her another mandarin. Then something interesting caught her eye. "Elsa-May look over there."

"That's Ryker, and isn't that the young man who followed us out of the Amish Dinner?"

Elsa-May turned around to look out the back of the buggy. "If you say so. I can't see that far away. It's just a blur."

"They look so alike. They look like brothers."

"*Nee,* Ettie. All young men look alike these days. It's the hair and the clothes."

"Hmmm. Could be."

"It was nice of the young man to come. You should speak to him, Ettie. Thank him for coming."

Ettie pointed to herself. "Me?"

"*Jah,* no one else is, and I can't. Unless you want me to go over there with my sore feet and with me feeling faint?"

Ettie inhaled deeply. "I'll go."

She walked over to the young man just as Ryker headed off. "Hello. I wanted to say thank you for coming. Did you know Deena well?"

"I remember you from the other day. I think I told

you then that I knew Deena. The Thripps asked me to be here to represent everyone at the store."

"That's very thoughtful of them." The golden nugget around his neck glinted in the sunlight. Ettie couldn't help noticing that gone was the thread that had tied the nugget to the chain. It had been replaced with a gold loop. "That's a nice gold piece around your neck."

He touched it with his fingers. "Thank you. I found it, panning."

"I didn't know there were any places to go panning around here."

"I go up north."

"It's an odd shape."

"They come in all kinds of shapes, no two are alike. Out of interest, do they know who killed Deena yet?" he asked.

"I'm not sure." She turned and looked at Ryker who was driving away. "Do you and Ryker know each other?" Ettie asked.

"I met him just now."

"You're not related? The two of you look very similar."

"No, we're not."

He stared at Ettie and Ettie had nothing left to say. "Well, thank you again for coming."

"No worries. How did you like your pickled pears?"

"Oh." Ettie chortled. "I haven't tried them yet."

"We won't be getting any more of them. I should go. Maybe I'll see you in the store sometime."

"Yes. You will."

Ettie smiled at him and walked back to Elsa-May.

When the funeral was over, Gabriel drove them to the police station and waited for them.

CHAPTER 26

"I'm sorry I couldn't make it to the funeral," Detective Kelly said, when the two sisters were seated in front of him. "I'm trying to get through this paperwork." He pointed to two tall piles of folders on his desk. "It never stops. I've got every available man on the Deena Brown case."

"Can't you get someone to do all that for you?" Elsa-May asked.

"I wish I could. But this is all information I need to deal with myself. Anyway, what brings you two in today, the day of the funeral? Don't you have a wake to attend?"

"Yes, but there was an interesting visitor at the funeral."

He lifted his arms, rested them on the desk, and leaned forward. "I'm listening."

"Ryker."

He sprang to his feet. "Where is he? We need to speak with him."

"Well, he was at the funeral," Elsa-May said.

"He was there today?"

"Yes."

"What kind of a car was he driving?"

Elsa-May shrugged her shoulders, while Ettie said, "I'm sorry, but I didn't take too much notice. I didn't even see a car at the bishop's house."

"Mrs. Smith, you could've told me earlier. I thought I was having a bad day, but this just tops it off."

"But what if she's a murderer?" Elsa-May asked.

"Who?"

"Deena," said Ettie. "Deena is the victim now, but many years ago, she might have been a killer. You see, Ryker told me a very interesting story."

He looked at his watch. "Just a moment. I need to get a car out to the graveyard to see if he's still around."

"I saw him leave. I couldn't tell you about the car. I didn't think it was important."

"We'll have to hope he came back once the crowd thinned."

They waited until Kelly made a couple of calls, and when he ended the last call, he sat down and placed his cell phone on the table. "Continue your story, Mrs. Smith."

Ettie repeated what Ryker had told her about Deena

and Hezekiah. Then she ended with, "And those were his very words, more or less."

"We can't just go there and start digging up the property unless we have a good reason. We certainly can't do it on hearsay. We were told he disappeared and until we learn anything to the contrary, the property still belongs to Hezekiah Lapp."

"He was many years older than Deena, wasn't he, Ettie?"

"Someone said he was nearly thirty years older."

Detective Kelly raised his eyebrows. "That's quite a big age difference. He'd be quite old by now."

"If he's still alive," said Ettie.

"I always thought of it as a marriage of convenience. What can people with a thirty-year age gap have in common?" Elsa-May's lips turned down at the corners.

"Generation gap. I didn't think you'd have one of those in your Amish community."

"Not so much, but each generation brings its own challenges."

"I'm sure it does."

"I asked Ryker to see you. I gave him your name," Ettie told him.

"I appreciate that. This was one time I should've been at that funeral. If it weren't for all the paperwork, I would've been." He looked up at them. "Do you want me to see if I can arrange for someone to drive you home?"

"Thank you, we'd appreciate that."

Ettie dug Elsa-May in the ribs. "Did you forget we have Gabriel waiting outside for us?"

"No. I thanked the detective and I was about to tell him that we wouldn't take him up on his kind offer. You jumped in and cut me off not allowing me to finish my words."

Kelly raised his eyebrows. "So, that's a 'no' to the ride home?"

"Yes," Ettie said.

Kelly frowned. "It's a yes?"

"I apologize for my confusing sister. She meant it's a no to the ride, but we thank you anyway," Elsa-May said.

"Very well. Keep finding out what you can and to keep you happy I'll check on the disappearance of Hezekiah Lapp. Call me immediately if you see Ryker again."

"We will and please let us know what you find out."

"Yes, I will." Kelly smiled and picked up his take-out coffee cup.

Ettie stood first and then helped Elsa-May up. As they walked out of the police station, Ettie was annoyed and it showed.

Elsa-May glanced over at her. "What's wrong with you?"

"You can never admit when you're wrong."

They were both halfway down the steps and Elsa-May hung onto the handrail and stopped. "When was I wrong?"

"You were going to have someone drive us home when you very well know we've got Gabriel waiting, and also, we'll have to go back to the bishop's house to make an appearance."

"Oh, Ettie. Why would I say yes to the ride home?"

"Because you forgot. Just admit it. You'd finished speaking and I didn't cut you off." Ettie pushed her lips together. She disliked it when Elsa-May made her look foolish.

"There's nothing to admit. You misunderstood what I said."

Ettie shook her head and kept walking down the steps. "Then you make out I'm stupid."

"I didn't. You said yes when you should've said no. You saw for yourself that even the detective was confused."

"I was correct when I said yes. He was the one who misunderstood me."

"I'll tell him that when I see him next, shall I?"

Ettie got to the pavement and turned around to look at her sister who was walking down the last two steps. "You made me look foolish, Elsa-May. You always do."

"Then perhaps..."

Ettie shook her finger at her. "Don't you say it because you'll be wrong. And we know how much you don't want to be wrong."

Elsa-May had taken her last step, then she put her hand over her mouth and chortled.

All Ettie could do was sigh.

Even though they were worn out, they decided that they'd go back to Bishop Paul and Mary's house. The community members and visitors had gathered for a meal after the funeral.

As they walked from the buggy to the house, Elsa-May whispered, "I can't get the image out of my mind."

"What image?"

"Deena hitting Hezekiah on the head with a frying pan. That poor boy witnessing that."

"If it's true." Ettie sighed. "It's not pleasant. I think we need to have a talk with Mary. She knows something, I'm sure of it."

"Me too, but not today, Ettie."

"Maybe not today, unless we get the opportunity."

When Ettie walked into the bishop's home, she looked at everybody wondering if one of them killed Deena. There was no one there that she suspected in the slightest and Ryker was nowhere about.

The whole time they were there, Mary avoided them. Every time they went near her, she moved somewhere else..

"How are you doing, Ettie?"

Ettie turned around to see Maggie, the gossip. "I'm fine, why?"

"You look worried."

Ettie sighed. "I'm just sad about Deena."

"We all are, but we have to member it was *Gott's* will. His ways are higher than our ways, and He knows the end from the beginning."

"I'll have to remember that."

"That's how I get through days like these."

Ettie followed Maggie's gaze to Luke, and then said, "It's nice for Annie to have Luke back."

Maggie's screwed up her nose. "I heard he wasn't at Clarks County like he said he was."

"Really?"

Maggie nodded.

"How do you know that?" Ettie asked.

"I have a cousin there. I inquired after him and John, my cousin, said he wasn't there. He would know because he's a deacon in the Clarks County community."

"That's odd."

"It is, and another thing that's odd is that Hezekiah disappeared all those years ago never to be heard from again. Someone could think some dark thoughts if they thought about it for too long."

Ettie had to ask. "What kind of thoughts?"

"That he was killed, but this isn't the time to think about things like that."

"I disagree. I think it's a very fitting time. If someone didn't murder her, we wouldn't be here. We know for sure that it wasn't an accident and that means somebody did that to her willingly and deliberately. Who do you think killed Hezekiah?"

Maggie shook her head. "It's not for me to say, but it's obvious when you think about it." Then she walked away.

Elsa-May and Gabriel walked over to Ettie.

Gabriel said, "What did you do to upset her, Ettie?"

"Who, Maggie?"

"Yes."

Ettie shook her head. "I was just talking about Deena." Ettie bit her lip. "Gabriel, do you think could you drive us to the exact place where you found Deena on the side of the road where her wheel got stuck?"

"Okay. I think I should be able to find the spot, if I walk over it. Do you want to go now?"

"Not now, when we finish here."

He smiled. "Sure. I can do that. Then after I take you home, I'll have to get organized for my trip. I'm leaving tomorrow."

CHAPTER 27

"Well here it is," Gabriel announced when he pulled up at the side of a lonely and isolated road.

From the buggy, Elsa-May looked around. "Nothing but trees here."

They all got out of the buggy. He pointed behind the parked buggy and then walked a few steps. "This is the area that her buggy wheel got caught. I had to fill the hole, then back up the horse, and then we got out."

"I can see the wheel marks." Ettie put her hands on her hips. "I wonder what she was doing out here all alone."

"Was she alone?" Elsa-May asked.

"She was when I came along," Gabriel told them.

"When did you see her?"

"I'm not sure of the exact day. I think it was Tuesday because I was helping Andrew look for missing cows."

"The bishop's son, Andrew?"

"That's the one. The back corner of the property isn't too far from here."

"I wonder if you were the last person to see her alive because they estimate that Tuesday was the day she died."

"No, Ettie, the killer would've been the last person to see her alive."

"The second last person to see her alive, then."

He shrugged. "That sent a shiver down my back just now. Who would want to kill a lovely lady like that? It just seems madness."

Ettie didn't tell him, but it was turning out that Deena might not have been what she seemed. Ettie spotted what looked like a trail between the trees and headed toward it.

"Where are you going, Ettie? You could fall down a rabbit hole and never find your way out again," Elsa-May called out.

"Wait up, Ettie. I'll come with you," Gabriel said.

Ettie didn't stop walking.

"I'm not going to stay here alone." Elsa-May caught up to them, despite her sore feet.

"I can see a path up ahead. I'm just seeing where it leads. You can go back and guard the horse and buggy so no one steals it, Elsa-May."

"Okay, but if I scream you better come running. The less I walk, the better."

"I know because you have skinny feet."

Elsa-May called back, "I was going to say it was because of the new shoes, but the problem is the skinny feet as well."

"And how is Selena?" Ettie asked when they were away from her sister.

"I haven't seen her in some time."

"Elsa-May and I thought for a while that there might have been a chance for you two."

"I don't think so. I don't think she would like a simple man like me."

"I thought you got on wonderfully with each other."

"Thanks, Ettie. There's always hope, isn't there?"

"There is always hope and there's also actions. Have you put any actions towards your hopes?"

"I would've if we didn't come from two different worlds."

"She started off in our world. And I've heard that how you've been raised never leaves you."

"We'll just have to see what *Gott's* will is for us."

"That's the best way."

"The main thing on my mind now is to rid myself of the house next door to you. Then I'll think about my other problems."

They came to a small clearing. "What's that building over there? It looks like a barn of sorts."

"This is the back of the bishop's property. It's an old barn. They probably don't use it. Over one hundred years ago, the old house was at this end of the property."

"How do you know these things?"

"A few years back, I was helping Andrew and the bishop strengthen the wall of that barn so it would last a bit longer."

"Is there anything in it?"

"I don't know. They used it for supplies years ago, but I don't know if they'd use it now. What exactly are you looking for, Ettie?"

"Clues. I'm looking for clues to find out who killed Deena."

"And you think that a clue would be in the barn?"

"No. Well… maybe. I'm just thinking that she must've pulled up on the roadside for some purpose, for some reason. Don't you think? She wasn't on the road, she was off the road. If she wasn't off the road, she wouldn't have got the wheel caught in the ditch."

"There could be any number of reasons."

"If she was meeting someone in that barn or storing something there, how else would she get to it?"

"The only way is past the bishop's house or on foot from the side-road where we've come just now."

"Exactly what I thought" Ettie started walking faster.

"What are you doing, Ettie? We can't go into the barn without permission."

Ettie stopped and turned around. "We can't?"

"Nee! And I'm running out of time. Perhaps you can ask Mary if you can have a look in the barn."

Ettie knew she couldn't do anything now. Not with

Gabriel being so upset about it. *"Denke,* for bringing us out. I think we've seen enough for today."

"I'll help you all I can when I get back. I might only be gone another couple of days."

"That would be nice but, hopefully, by then we'll already know who killed Deena."

Once Gabriel had delivered the elderly sisters home safely, the two sisters sat in their living room.

"Ettie, we must talk with Andrew and ask him what he took out of Deena's barn."

"We shouldn't. We should look in his old barn and see if whatever it is, is there."

"Break in?" Elsa-May asked.

"Yes. We can't ask him because how would we explain that we saw him with the object? We can't tell him we were hiding in Deena's house watching him take something out of Deena's barn."

"I see. That could be a problem. He must've seen us at the window or thought he saw us. He came in saying 'hello, hello,' remember?"

"That's kind of hard to forget." Ettie tapped on her chin. "What we'll do is look in the old barn, the one we discovered today. If Andrew is trying to hide it, he might've put it there. That makes sense to me. I would've looked inside when we were there, but Gabriel had a strong reaction to it."

"Hmm. I don't know, Ettie. It might be a waste of time. We're thinking it's a clue to Deena's murder or perhaps a body, but it might be nothing at all. It could be something he's already used, like supplies of some kind. Maybe it was something he sold, or something he gave to someone else. It might have simply been an old rug. There are thousands of things he could've done with whatever it was. That's why I think we should ask him."

Ettie sighed. "Why don't we look first and if there's nothing there, then we'll ask him?"

"Okay. I'll agree with that because I won't get any peace until I do. We'll set out first thing tomorrow, okay?"

Ettie licked her lips. "Why not tonight?"

"In the dark?"

"Jah."

"From what you said, Gabriel won't drive us."

"I don't think we should involve him with breaking into the bishop's barn."

"Let's just think about it for a while and see what happens. Let's have something to eat first. Have our dinner and see if we still feel like doing it tonight."

"Very well."

"Your turn to cook the evening meal, Ettie."

Ettie rubbed her hands together. "What can I do with the pickled pears?"

Elsa-May turned up her nose. "I was thinking chicken, gravy and baked vegetables. That's what I feel like."

"I think pickled pears are something you'd eat with

something else. You'd have to cut them finely, I'd think."

"Ettie, less thinking about food and more doing something about food, like cooking it."

Ettie pushed herself to her feet. She didn't bother telling Elsa-May she wasn't thinking of preparing a meal of pickled pears. That would be ridiculous. Sometimes it was better to keep quiet and not have a conversation about things. When she walked into the kitchen she saw the jar of pears on the center of the table, atop the half-completed jigsaw puzzle. Ettie ignored her irritation over the puzzle and picked up the jar. She turned it over and read the back.

Gluten free.

Ingredients: Pears, apple, sugar, cinnamon, juniper, bay leaves.

Serving suggestions. These tart and tangy pears are delicious served with a cheeseboard or simply with creamed cheese. Or add to your muesli or breakfast cereal, or simply toss in a salad.

In even smaller writing were the words, *made by DB.*

"D.B. Elsa-May, these pickled pears were made by Deena Brown."

Elsa-May walked into the kitchen. "They were?"

"It says made by D.B. Deena Brown. It doesn't say Deena Brown, but D and B are her initials."

"You could be right, Ettie, and if you are, it would be a first."

Ettie ignored her sister's comment and opened the

lid to smell the contents. They smelled spicy, like peppercorns.

"May I get back to my knitting now?"

"You may."

Elsa-May walked out of the room. A few minutes later, she called out, "I'm not hearing any cooking sounds."

"Don't you worry about it. I'll have a meal on the table in an hour." She looked down at the puzzle. "Well, on part of the table."

Ettie popped the jar of pickled pears in the cupboard and set about preparing the meal.

Over dinner that night, Elsa-May brought up another subject. "You know what we need to do, Ettie?"

"What?"

"Clean the house next door. I think it wasn't clean enough and that's why those people weren't interested. I remember he said it was dusty and I was embarrassed."

"I don't think it was that. I think it was the murder. No one wants to live in a place where someone was killed."

"That was a long time ago."

Ettie shook her head. "It wasn't that long ago."

"Long enough."

"Do we have to clean it? I'm sure it will be fine. I'll just open up some windows and get some fresh air into the rooms."

"And do you think it will blow the dirt out with it?"

Ettie smiled. "That's what I'm hoping."

"No, Ettie, you're just being lazy."

Ettie's mouth turned down at the corners. "I prefer to think of it as conserving my energy. We have our own place to clean and our own things to do. Isn't it enough that we'll be showing prospective buyers through the house while trying to solve a murder?"

"You remember what our father always used to say. If a job is worth doing…"

"I know, but we really didn't have any choice in this job. I don't even know that we'll be any good at it."

"Just leave it to me, then."

"What, the cleaning? *Wunderbaar.*"

"*Nee,* the selling."

"Oh."

"I'm good at selling. I sell a lot whenever we have to sell anything at the charity events. I always have the top sales."

"That's because you talk so much that people buy from you so they can move on. Otherwise, they'd be there all day."

Elsa-May smiled. "I think you're a tiny bit upset that I'm better than you at some things—most things. But that's okay, we can't all be good at everything."

"Are you saying you're one of the people who are good at everything?"

"I'm not saying that. That would be prideful. Why

don't you stay home when the next people come here to see the house?"

"Maybe. I didn't think we had to talk about price with them, do we? He already knows the price he wants for it."

"They can always pay more."

"No, it will be hard to get a buyer for this place. Everyone will remember what happened here if they live around these parts."

"Perhaps you should buy it," Elsa-May suggested, "and then we could live side-by-side."

"We already thought about that last time it was for sale, remember? We decided against it. We have a perfectly good house that suits the two of us."

"It was just an idea. Let's go take another look at it."

Ettie sighed. "I don't want to. We have too many other things to do."

"We can do them later."

"Elsa-May, you said you'd go to the bishop's barn with me tonight."

Elsa-May shook her head. "I said, I might. I believe I said I'd see how I felt. Right now, I don't feel like it."

"I'll go myself, then."

"Fine, you go by yourself, but I just want you to come with me next door first. We won't clean tonight, Ettie, we'll take a look and see what needs doing. It will only take a minute or two."

Reluctantly, Ettie agreed.

A few minutes later, Elsa-May put the key in the front door of the house next door. When she pushed it open, they were engulfed in stale air.

"You were correct about needing fresh air in here, Ettie. Let's go throughout and open the windows."

As Ettie walked one way and Elsa-May another, Ettie called out, "I wonder why Gabriel is going to Luzerne County? Perhaps to visit a lady friend?"

"If he is, he's being tight-lipped about it." Elsa-May had opened the last one of her half of the windows, and she started brushing dust off the furniture with her fingertips. Then she stared at her fingertips in fright. "Look how black everything is."

Ettie joined her in the living room. "The place does need a good cleaning. But how are we going to have time as well as talk to people about Deena's murder, and take a look in the bishop's barn?" Ettie sighed and slumped onto the couch. "Many things about Deena don't add up."

Elsa-May brushed off the couch beside Ettie and then sat down. "Let's talk it out. Just think of it as a big puzzle. At the moment, we are gathering all the pieces and when we're done gathering we can sit down and fit the pieces together. Starting at the edges."

Ettie made a face at her sister. "The edges?"

"Yes, you always start with the edges because you know they're straight."

"I don't see how that compares with a murder. What are the straight edges in a murder case?"

"The straight pieces and the four corners are the facts we know. We know Deena is dead. We know how she died. We know who didn't do it and we… whatever we know, then those are the straight edges and the corners."

"That's very good, I like it."

Elsa-May's face lit up. "I'll have to tell Detective Kelly that next time. I think that will help him solve his cases."

Ettie stifled a laugh before she responded. "I can't wait for you to tell him. And I just want to ask one thing of you."

"What's that?"

"Just be sure that I'm there when you say it to him." It was true—Ettie couldn't wait to see the look on his face. "Okay let's think it through. Luke wasn't in Ohio, according to Maggie. Did Luke take revenge for his brother's death and kill Deena? If he wasn't in Ohio, he could've been close by, hiding out."

"You didn't tell me Luke wasn't in Ohio."

"Oh—sorry. That's what Maggie told me. Then there's Ryker. He hated Deena, and blamed her for everything."

Elsa-May nodded. "Yes, and then there's Mrs. Thripp. Could she have believed the rumors about her husband and Deena and killed Deena in a jealous rage?"

"Then there's Mr. Thripp himself. We heard him tell Deena he was sorry. Sorry for what, for killing her?

Then there's Wayne. Perhaps Wayne killed her because he was also upset by the Mr. Thripp rumors."

"Don't forget Andrew," Elsa-May said.

"Andrew?"

"*Jah,* he could've wanted whatever was in her barn. With her dead, he could take it."

Ettie frowned. "I'm not so sure about that. We don't even know what it was yet. And that's why we should go there now and not waste time."

"Then there is someone from her past. Ryker's father. He might've sent someone to kill her."

"But why now?"

"I don't know. I'm just naming all the people who might've wanted her out of the way."

Ettie tapped a finger on her chin. "I keep coming back to the old barn at the bishop's house. Deena told Gabriel she was out that way sketching, but she wasn't a sketcher, as far as we know. If she was, wouldn't there be drawings and drawing supplies somewhere in her house? We saw nothing like that."

"That's true, Ettie. Okay, you win."

"Good! What do I get?"

"My agreement. We'll go to that crumbling-down old barn tonight to see what we can find."

Ettie clapped her hands together. "Excellent."

"We should head there now."

"You're coming with me?"

"I am, against my better judgment." Elsa-May pushed herself to her feet and Ettie followed her to the door. They locked up and headed home with their way lit by flashlights.

When they walked through the door of their home, Ettie said, “How will we get there?”

“We’ll have to call a taxi. We can have it wait for us where Deena’s buggy wheel got caught.”

Ettie grimaced. “We’ll have to walk through all those trees in the dark.”

“It won’t be in the dark because we’ll have flashlights.”

Ettie knew she’d have to agree and get moving before Elsa-May changed her mind. “Let’s put our coats on and head down to the shanty. I'll grab extra batteries, just in case.”

CHAPTER 28

Ettie and Elsa-May got out of the taxi, but not before Elsa-May made sure that the driver would wait for them.

They were both armed with flashlights. "Good thing I heard that Bishop Paul and Mary have been invited out for dinner every night this week."

"That's good. There's no chance of them seeing our lights, then."

"Unless Andrew sees them, but I'm sure you can't possibly see this barn from their house. He also might've gone with them."

Ettie looked up at the sky and said a silent prayer of thanks that the moon was also helping to light their way. It wasn't as dark as it could've been.

"Not far now," Elsa-May said over her shoulder.

"That's good because I hate to think what the taxi driver will charge us. We must be quick."

Elsa-May put her hand on the old wooden barn door and pushed it open. "There might be nothing here at all."

When the door fully opened, they saw it wasn't empty. The bishop's family had been using the barn for extra storage.

"Oh, Elsa-May, how are we going to find anything among all this?"

"I see it, Ettie."

Elsa-May moved in and not wanting to be left behind, Ettie hung onto the back of her sister's apron. "What is it?"

"Look there, Ettie."

When Elsa-May came to a stop, Ettie looked where her sister's flashlight was focused.

"Good work, Elsa-May. That's what Andrew took from Deena's barn."

"Well, I have an apology to make to you."

"You do, but that can wait. Right now, we must see what this bundle holds."

"Wait, Ettie. What if it's the worst thing that we thought about?"

Ettie knew that Elsa-May meant Hezekiah's body. "We'll have to see. If we don't, and it is what we thought, it might lay here undiscovered for years."

Ettie sighed. "Go ahead, open it."

"Me?"

The vision of the taxi's meter ticking upward loomed before Ettie's eyes. "Okay, I'll do it. Move out of the way." While Elsa-May shone the light for her, Ettie unwound the rope from around the long parcel.

It wasn't a body.

"What is it, Ettie?"

"Shine the flashlight on it and hold it still so I can see. I put mine down somewhere and can't see it. Wait, I just found it." Ettie grabbed the end of the flashlight and shone it. "Oh, no, Elsa-May. It's just a shovel, a pick, and a frying pan. It looks like Ryker might be right and…"

"You know what this means, Ettie?"

"I do."

"Andrew is a thief."

"What?" Ettie shone her flashlight in Elsa-May's face to see her shaking her head in disgust. "*Nee.* Think about it. Why would he steal these? Remember what Ryker said Deena did to Hezekiah? Hit him over the head! The shovel and the pick, well, we can only imagine what she used them for."

Elsa-May's eyes grew wide. "Do you think this is the very same frypan? It's so large. It would weigh a ton. There's no handle on it. She might've hit him so hard she broke the handle. No wonder Hezekiah left and never came back."

"No! This points to Ryker telling the truth about Hezekiah being killed."

"That's what I meant."

Ettie narrowed her eyes at her sister. "You said that's why Hezekiah left and never came back."

"He left, meaning he was murdered and of course, he couldn't come back after he died even though some people such as Mr. Thripp think they can communicate with the dead."

It was no use. Her sister would never admit to being wrong. "To me, this proves something else as well," Ettie said.

"What?"

"I'm not sure yet, but it'll come to me."

"Let's sit down and think about it." Elsa-May wasted no time sitting on a bale of hay and Ettie sat next to her. "Andrew knew these things were in Deena's barn, Ettie, but how?"

"Perhaps someone told him."

"Obviously, but who?"

Ettie nibbled on a fingernail while she thought.

"Ryker?" Ettie suggested.

"Possibly, but that doesn't make much sense. No, Elsa-May, when you have a son, you make the son do things." Ettie tapped a finger on her chin. "Mary!"

"Are you saying Mary knew it was there and got Andrew to bring it here?"

Ettie nodded. "Exactly. She asked her son to fetch it just like you order your sons and grandsons about."

"I do not! Anyway, what makes you think Mary is involved?"

"Deena might have shared her secret of what really happened. She might have confessed what she did. Did you think of that? I knew Mary knew more," Ettie said.

"She said something about a dark secret and this was the darkest secret anyone could ever have. Mary was keeping that secret for Deena, even when Deena had died."

"Well, what will we do now? If we take these things away, we'll be tampering with evidence and Detective Kelly will be angry with us." Elsa-May cringed at the thought of an angry detective.

"I know and if we do nothing then nothing happens and we never learn the truth."

"Looks like you'll have to call Detective Kelly, Ettie. It's the only way."

Ettie sighed. "I can't do that either because then everyone will know that we came to this barn uninvited."

"Wait a minute. There is another way. We could do a prank call."

"Oh, you mean like an anonymous call?"

"*Jah*. That's the one."

"That's a great idea. We'll call from the shanty when we get back home. We'll call the police station and say we found something suspicious that might be connected with Deena Brown's murder, and it was hidden in the old barn at the back of the bishop's property."

"Okay."

With her foot, Ettie flipped over the burlap sack material to cover what they'd found inside.

"Why did he bring it here, Ettie?"

"I don't know, but I don't think members of the bishop's family would be involved in a murder." Ettie sighed. "Like I said before, Mary knows something."

When the taxi drove them to the shanty near where they lived, Ettie had her hand on the phone's receiver. "I can't do it."

"I'm not doing it. Don't look at me." Elsa-May shook her head.

"I think we should give Mary a chance to explain why it was there," Ettie said.

"Did it occur to you that she might not know anything about it? It might be something to do with Andrew. Or do you have one of those hunches again?"

Ettie shook her head. "First thing in the morning, let's visit Mary."

"Nee! You must make the call, Ettie. Do it!"

Ettie's mouth turned down at the corners. "Do I have to?"

Half an hour later, Elsa-May got so impatient with Ettie that she made the anonymous call to the police station herself.

Elsa-May spoke in a deep voice. "I'd like to report something about the Deena Brown case. The murder weapon is in the Amish bishop's barn, wrapped in a burlap sack. Not the normal barn, the one at the back of the property." And then she hung up. "Oh, Ettie, that was dreadful. I don't know why you couldn't have done it."

"One of us had to. Let's go home. Snowy will be

wondering where we've gotten to. We're never usually out this late."

"I am tired, and—"

"My feet hurt," Ettie finished Elsa-May's sentence for her.

"Well, they do."

"I'm not carrying you."

Elsa-May chuckled. "It would be nice if you could."

"For one of us, anyway."

CHAPTER 29

Ettie and Elsa-May sat eating oatmeal for breakfast when a knock sounded on their door. Snowy went crazy, barking while turning in circles.

"It's Detective Kelly. You put Snowy in your room and I'll answer the door." Ettie put her half-eaten bowl of food by the sink and headed out of the kitchen. When she opened the door and saw Kelly's smiling face, she knew there'd been a breakthrough in the case.

"How are you on this bright and lovely morning, Mrs. Smith?"

"Fine. Do come in."

Elsa-May said, "Morning, Detective Kelly. I've just locked Snowy away, so no need to worry."

When they were all seated, Ettie asked, "Has something happened with Deena's case? You're looking rather pleased this morning."

"Many things. We had a couple of anonymous tips come through last night and we're following those leads."

"Good."

"We've also found Deena's shoe. It was in some tall grass about a mile up the road. We've sent it off for analysis. Also, we've arrested Ryker Lapp. Although I'm sure you know by now that Lapp isn't his real, legal name, he still goes by that name, unofficially."

"So, he murdered Deena?" Elsa-May asked.

"Yes. Although he denies it up to this point. My men are still questioning him, hoping for an admission." He looked at his watch and then looked up and smiled. "I might have five or ten minutes to spare."

Ettie and Elsa-May got comfortable and then stared at the detective.

"Ryker went back to work like it was any other day and that's where we picked him up."

"How do you know he did it?" Elsa-May asked.

Kelly shook his head. "From his cell phone records, we know he was in the vicinity of Deena's house around the time the coroner's report says she was murdered. We also found a tire track at her house that matches those on his car. He's telling some huge stories. I only hope that doesn't get him off if he persuades his lawyer to back him in that line of defense."

"What is he saying?" Ettie asked.

"He's saying he visited, but he never killed her.

Then he told us a fanciful story that twisted the whole thing around to his poor mother killing Hezekiah Lapp, the man who went missing."

"So he's saying Deena killed Hezekiah?"

"Yes, but that tells us that Ryker most likely killed Hezekiah as well as Deena. He's a liar just like his birth father. He's killed two people and so has his father, even though his father was only convicted for one murder and that was downgraded to manslaughter."

"How do you know Ryker killed Hezekiah, too?"

"I will have concrete proof as soon as I get the forensic results on some implements that were found after we got a call to the station."

Ettie couldn't even look at Elsa-May. "That's quite unbelievable."

"That was convenient," Elsa-May said.

He looked at Elsa-May for a lengthy moment, and then stared at Ettie. "I listened to the recording of that call."

"You did?" Elsa-May coughed.

"I did. It sounded like someone was trying to make their voice deeper. Anyway, thank you."

Ettie froze. He knew it was one of them.

"It's a sad story for Deena," Kelly said. "That poor woman took the child into the Amish community after his mother was killed in a drive-by shooting. Enrico Garcia, more commonly known as Rico Garcia, wanted a better life for his son, so paid his bookkeeper, Deena Brown, to take him far away and raise him out of harm's way. He never knew where she went, but he kept providing for them both by having the money go into her bank account every week until the boy was eighteen."

"He must've trusted Deena."

"I'd dare say she was more than his bookkeeper. It's possible she was involved somehow in his crooked dealings, but that's not what I'm investigating. I'll leave that be."

Elsa-May nodded. "You said she thought the boy would have a better life in our community?"

"That's what I'm guessing. With his mother killed, it was only natural a father would want the boy to get away and have a different life, but the old debate over nature or nurture came into play. I guess nature won. Ryker is as bad as his father. His father is a criminal and the apple didn't fall far from the tree. We just hope he won't get bail when he goes before a judge tomorrow morning."

"His father murdered people, is that what you said before?" Elsa-May asked.

Kelly scoffed. "He got charged for manslaughter. The man's got a list of offenses as long as my arm. He's done everything under the sun and then some."

"I can see why Deena wanted to get the boy away from that life," Ettie said.

"We now have a warrant to look for Hezekiah's body on his and Deena's property. We've been there since sunup."

"Thanks for letting us know."

Kelly's cell phone rang. "Excuse me. I'm sorry. I didn't know I had this with me. I usually leave it in the car when I come into your house." He stood. "I'll take this call outside."

When Kelly walked out, Ettie and Elsa-May sat in silence.

"What are you thinking, Ettie?"

"Something's unsettling me. If Ryker killed Deena, how did the evidence end up with Andrew and how did Mary even know about it?"

"Or did Mary know about it at all? You're assuming she knew. The only thing we know for sure is that Andrew knew about it."

"That's true. And, why was Mr. Thripp telling Deena he was sorry? Why did everyone keep thinking someone was in Deena's house?"

"Besides all that, where is Hezekiah's body? If he's dead, surely he would've shown up somewhere long before now."

"If there's any truth to what Ryker said, we might have the answer to that soon."

Because he was just outside the front door, Ettie and Elsa-May heard Detective Kelly when he raised his voice. "You found *what?*"

Elsa-May shook her head, and whispered, "I hope they didn't find poor old Hezekiah."

"It sounds like they found something else, something pretty shocking."

A minute later, Kelly walked back through the door. "I'll have to go."

Elsa-May pushed herself to her feet. "What is it?"

Ettie stood too. "Did they dig up something at Deena's house?"

He took a few steps closer. "The only thing they found was a tin of small gold nuggets that was buried close to the house. The dog came up with nothing."

"No body?" Elsa-May asked.

"Not as yet, but they're still digging. Hezekiah's brother was kind enough to provide us with something of Hezekiah's for the sniffer dog. I was sure that we'd find him, if any of the stories were true." Kelly turned around and walked out the door without even saying goodbye.

The sisters sat down.

"Luke is being strangely helpful," Ettie said. "And when was the last time we saw a gold nugget?"

Elsa-May gasped. "Around the young man's neck who works at the Amish Diner. Oh dear, now you've got me saying it wrong. I meant Amish *Dinner.*"

"Correct on both counts." Ettie tapped her finger on her chin. "And that young man was at Deena's funeral, too."

"You told me he said he was there on behalf of the—"

"What a coincidence." Ettie stood up.

"Where are you going?"

"I've got so many things to organize. It'll be a long

day. We're going to find a killer, and we're going to make inroads into selling the house next door, but first, I must finish my oatmeal."

Elsa-May stood. "While you do that, I'll let poor Snowy out of the bedroom, and then I'll finish my breakfast as well. It sounds as though I'll need it."

CHAPTER 30

The very next night, Ettie hosted an open house event at Gabriel's place next door. She'd invited several people and at short-notice she had employed the people from the Amish Dinner to cater the event.

Earlier in the day, Ettie had gone into town by herself, and Elsa-May had cleaned Gabriel's house for the occasion.

The house was glowing with a combination of soft candlelight and the soft gas lighting that Gabriel had previously installed.

Kelly's men had found no body buried at Deena's property, but they had brought in a metal detector and uncovered another small tin of gold nuggets.

Mrs. Thripp and her daughter, Sally, had the table spread with tempting and tasty-looking treats.

Just as Ettie had planned, there were no members of

the general public in attendance, only everyone who had been close to Deena.

After all of them had looked around the house and people had started eating, Ettie cleared her throat.

"I told everyone this was a special event. Apart from showcasing the potential of this lovely home, tonight, a murderer will be exposed."

A deathly hush swept over the guests, until Maggie Overberg spoke in a squeaky voice.

"Deena Brown's murderer?"

"Yes." Ettie looked at the employee from Amish Dinner, whom she'd also invited to the open house. "Gregory."

He looked up. "Don't look at me. I didn't kill anyone."

"You harassed Deena Brown constantly. For those who don't know, gold nuggets were found buried outside Deena's house."

"Two tins of them," Elsa-May interjected.

Ettie continued, "Yesterday I made a trip to the local gold buyer in town and found out that Deena regularly sold small gold nuggets. Someone was giving them to her."

"Who?" Maggie asked.

"I'll get to that in a moment." Ettie again focused her attention on the young man. "Deena relented to your constant harassment and gave you money here and there, and I wouldn't be surprised if you were the one who ransacked her home when she died, looking for money. In doing so, you found some nuggets she hadn't gotten around to burying."

"That's not true."

"I notice the nugget you're wearing today is properly fitted with a gold loop. The other day at the store when I first met you, it was tied to your chain with string. That is evidence that you recently acquired it and hastily tied it to your chain. The day of the funeral, I noticed it was properly fitted."

"It's not true. I told you I found it."

"And that was probably true. You found it... inside Deena's home. Do you admit to visiting Deena regularly?"

"To be honest, I would say I did, but only about work."

"The same gold buyer has you on his CCTV footage selling gold nuggets the very day after Deena would've died. Do you mind saying where you got them?"

He looked around the room, and then said, "I just found them."

"Maybe Deena said no to you and said she'd tell Mr. Thripp about your bullying, or perhaps she threatened to tell the police. On that day, you went too far and you killed her."

"I didn't. Okay, I took some gold, but I didn't kill her."

Ettie took a deep breath and turned her attention to the bishop's wife. "Mary, the police found some things in your barn that they thought were suspicious. Tell me how they got there."

"Oh, those things? I told the police about that. A while after Hezekiah disappeared, Deena told me I could take his old gold-panning equipment. When Andrew brought it back to the house there was only a shovel, a pick, and a gold pan. I asked Andrew to get rid of them. They were no use to me. I thought Hezekiah would have one of those metal detectors. I didn't even know that Andrew didn't toss those things away. I just found out he'd stored it in the old barn with everything else."

Andrew frowned. "I was going to throw it away, *Mamm*, so I put it with the other junk for a later time."

"What would you want with a metal detector, Mary?" Maggie asked.

"To find things dropped by our ancestors on our property from years ago, old tools and such. It's fascinating what can be found."

"Ettie, you were wrong about quite a few things. You must be feeling foolish," Elsa-May said.

Ettie *was* a little. What they thought was a frypan was an old metal gold-panning bowl. She pressed on. "Andrew, I wonder why you walked into Deena's house after she died and expected someone to be there."

He looked away. "I thought Ryker might've been there."

"Why? There was no car outside. Where would he have put his car?"

"He might not have come there in a car. He could've arrived by taxi." Andrew shrugged. "How did you know—"

Elsa-May held her hand up. "Ettie is the one doing the asking tonight. Continue, Ettie."

Andrew said, "Let me just say I thought Ryker might've been in the house and that's all I can tell you. I overheard Annie telling *Mamm* that the last time she went to Deena's house, she thought she heard someone inside. I added up the days and now everyone knows Deena wouldn't have been there. I had a hunch it might've been Ryker."

At that moment, Gabriel walked into the house and gave Ettie a nod.

"Gabriel and I have a big surprise for everyone."

Everyone turned to look at Gabriel and then he stepped aside. A much older and grayer Hezekiah walked into the room.

Annie jumped to her feet. "Hezekiah, is that you?"

Luke walked up to his brother. "Hezekiah!"

The brothers hugged.

"Where have you been?" Annie asked.

"I've been in Hazelton, over in Luzerne County. I have a small toy store specializing in puzzles. Ettie sent Gabriel into the store and he recognized me." He looked at the bishop. "I'm sorry, but I hadn't agreed with the *Ordnung* for years before I left, and I wanted to live an authentic life. Once I left, it was easier just to stay away. I didn't want to have to explain and I didn't want Deena to have to explain anything."

Ettie said, "Deena knew Hezekiah was still alive and she supported his decision to leave. He was able to help Deena by giving her cash and, every so often, some gold nuggets that she could sell as needed."

"I never was one to trust bank accounts. I hear she buried most of the nuggets," Hezekiah said. "I didn't know she was doing that."

"Oh, Gabriel, about that time she got her buggy wheel caught…" Elsa-May said, letting her voice trail off questioningly.

Gabriel nodded. "Hezekiah told me that's where they met. It was an out of the way place where no one else would see them. He wanted to remain undiscovered."

"Ettie, you said a killer would be revealed, so who's the killer?" Elsa-May urged. "It's not you, is it, Hezekiah?"

"It's not. Ryker drove to see me the day he heard that she died."

"You kept in contact with Ryker?" Elsa-May asked.

"Always. He knew where I was the whole time."

Ettie faced Mrs. Thripp. "There were rumors about your husband and Deena, but they were totally unwarranted."

Mrs. Thripp pursed her lips. "I didn't kill her, if that's what you think."

"Ryker told some tall stories about Deena, the

woman who raised him. He showed his friends that she had a shelf for her food and a shelf for Hezekiah's and his food."

"She did," Hezekiah said. "It wasn't that she was eating better food and giving us sub-standard food. She had to eat separately because she was—"

"Gluten intolerant," Ettie finished his sentence for him. "Ryker lied about Deena hitting you over the head with a frying pan, Hezekiah."

Hezekiah gasped. "He said that about his loving mother?"

Ettie nodded. "I'm afraid so."

A hush of silence hung over the room.

"I know he didn't kill her," Hezekiah said. "They didn't get along, but he still kept in contact with her over the years."

Maggie Overberg said, "Well, Ettie, who did it? Was it Ryker?"

Ettie said, "Nothing about Deena's death made sense to me until I removed some things from my head, just like you can't make sense of a puzzle if you have some pieces in front of you that belong to a different puzzle. So, I removed the things that were possibly untrue, and didn't belong. Annie, you said from the start that Deena was fearful about a man from her past coming to get her, but no such man existed, did he?"

Annie nodded. "That's correct.

Ettie continued, "If the man had existed, I'm sure

Deena would've told the bishop or Mary about him. Also, you wrote that note pretending it came from Deena and you also said Deena asked you to make it look like she was home when she wasn't."

"Why did you do all of that, Annie?" Mary asked.

"I'll tell you why," Ettie said. "Annie heard Ryker's stories about Deena killing Hezekiah." Ettie looked directly at Annie. "You thought Luke heard that same story and that he killed Deena out of revenge for her killing Hezekiah."

"An eye for an eye," Maggie said. "I can see how you might've thought that, Annie."

"Annie, you were covering up for your husband unnecessarily. Luke didn't kill Deena."

Luke's mouth dropped open and he stared at Annie. "You thought I killed Deena, my own *schweschder*-in-law?"

"I didn't know. You were so upset about Hezekiah. I tried to keep those rumors from you. I only had Maggie at the house when you weren't there."

Maggie huffed. "I don't know what you're saying. Are you saying I would've repeated those stories about Deena?"

"Sorry, Maggie." A tear trickled down Annie's face. "I'm wrong whatever I do. I'm guilty. Guilty of burying her. Okay, you want to know… I'll tell you."

"That would be *gut!*" the bishop stated firmly.

"I came home and saw her body at the front of the house. I thought the worst possible thing happened. I thought Luke had killed her. He was due home, but he didn't show. I knew I wouldn't be strong enough to move her and I had to do something before someone drove past and saw her body there."

"What did you do?" Elsa-May asked.

"I got a shovel and covered her over with dirt until she couldn't be seen. I know it was wrong."

"Why would you think I did that when I wasn't even there?" Luke asked.

"If you remember correctly, it happened on the day you were due home. That's why I thought it was you and when it got late in the day and on into the next day, and you still weren't home, I was sure that you'd killed her and pretended to still be away. Maggie said something about you not being where you were supposed to be."

"I was."

"I heard that you weren't. I asked my cousin."

"Your cousin is wrong. Neither of you should be spreading such stories."

"Ettie, who did it?" Mary urged.

"Yes, Ettie," Maggie said, ignoring Luke's rebuke, "we're all dying to know."

CHAPTER 31

"Gregory, you didn't tell the whole truth just now. You were at the gold seller cashing in nuggets, but most of them were on behalf of your boss. Deena was loaning money to you, Mr. Thripp, as a friend, and Deena didn't know you were sending Gregory to harass her for even more money."

Gregory opened his mouth but said nothing.

Mrs. Thripp frowned at her husband. "What's she saying?"

Mr. Thripp. "I've got no idea. She's mad."

"Tell them it's not so, Dad," Sally said.

"Let me tell a story," Ettie said. "I did some research at the library yesterday. I read how hard it is to find gold and how exciting it is for the prospector to find a gold nugget. Imagine taking those precious pieces and giving them to someone who had little regard for the sweat and the tears that went into finding them."

Everyone was silent.

Ettie continued, "Hezekiah. You found out that after you'd been giving Deena money for years that it was being leeched by the Thripps. You confronted Deena about it and the two of you got into a terrible argument. Why don't you tell me about the last time you saw your wife alive?"

"We met at the usual place. She'd called a few days before and asked me for cash. She said a friend needed sixteen thousand dollars to expand his business and he'd pay it back in six months. I said I'd meet her. I might've led her to believe I was bringing the money, but I was really meeting her to find out more about this 'friend.' I drove to our usual spot, but she never arrived. I drove to her place to see if she was there, and on the way I saw her walking near Annie and Luke's house. I stopped and asked her why she hadn't come to meet me."

"What did she say?" Elsa-May asked.

"Her horse was lame and the phone in her barn wasn't working. She was on her way to Mary's place to use the phone in her barn so she could call me."

"So, you got into an argument about the money and then killed her?" Maggie asked.

"No. Deena got into my car and we talked. I insisted she tell me the truth about this friend. She eventually told me it was the man who owned Amish Dinner."

Everyone gasped and looked at Mr. Thripp.

"The other thing she said was she needed me to resurface, show myself, and then divorce her. Deena wanted to be free to marry again."

Ettie wasn't sure who Deena had wanted to marry. Would the bishop allow her to marry Wayne, or was she considering leaving the community to marry Mr. Thripp, who might have possibly led her to believe he'd divorce his current wife? "Then what happened?"

"I left her there and drove home. She was upset with me because I said I would not give her money for her friends, and I also told her I wouldn't agree to the divorce. Now I regret refusing her the divorce. Our relationship was over, but I never believed in divorce. I suppose that's selfish of me. She said some horrible things. She said she was glad I left and that I was never a proper husband. And, maybe I wasn't."

"So you picked up a rock and hit her over the head?" Elsa-May asked.

"No. I never killed her, but I was angry. Like I said, I got in my car and drove away."

"Did you see anyone else about?" Elsa-May asked.

"No, but her place was on my route home and I did see the Amish Dinner van parked outside."

"That's a lie!" Mr. Thripp called out.

Ettie's eyes grew wide. "How would you know that unless you knew the exact day that she died?"

"I didn't. I was guessing. Everyone's out to make

me look guilty. The van hasn't been near her place for weeks."

"Mr. Thripp, you expected Deena to call you after her meeting with Hezekiah, to make arrangements to deliver you the cash, but she never called. You got angry and went looking for her. You must've found her just after Hezekiah left. You were enraged she had no money for you and you killed her."

His bottom lip trembled.

"What would you say if I told you the police have evidence that shows you were with her the day she died?" Ettie asked.

He frowned. "She came at me. It was self-defense."

"Be quiet, stupid," Mrs. Thripp snapped. "Don't say a thing. Let's go."

"Not so fast," Detective Kelly stepped through the doorway and stood in front of them. "Maximus Thripp, I'm arresting you for the murder of Deena Brown."

While he snapped the cuffs on him, his wife wailed her protests. Sally stood there, stunned.

Kelly had police waiting outside who took over from him and placed Thripp in a van.

"Get all our food and our plates, and meet me at the car," Mrs. Thripp snapped at Sally.

Sally sprang into action and started clearing away what was left of the food.

Ettie walked up to Hezekiah, and whispered, "Thanks for helping me out just now by saying his van was at the house."

"It's the least I could do. I can't help feeling all this could have been avoided. Deena was lonely. Our marriage was based on a friendship and if I'd said yes to a divorce, things might've been different. She might have married Wayne."

Wayne, who was standing behind Hezekiah had overheard. "She wanted to marry me?"

Hezekiah turned around. "She did. Yes."

Wayne's mouth turned down and he wiped away a tear.

Maggie managed to grab the last of the hot finger-food pies before they disappeared into the trash. "Ettie, you knew Mr. Thripp killed her?"

"I only figured it out recently. Well, I thought it before, but I didn't have the proper pieces in front of me."

Ettie sat down next to Elsa-May. Everyone was talking with one another while Gregory helped Sally pack everything up.

"I'm sorry about this," Gregory said to Ettie over his shoulder as he headed out the door.

"Adjust the catering invoice when you send it to us," Elsa-May called after him.

He stopped walking. "I think I can safely say you won't be charged."

"In that case..." Elsa-May sprang to her feet and grabbed the very last cucumber sandwich even as Sally grabbed the plate out from underneath her hand.

Ettie's heart was gladdened when she saw Luke and

Hezekiah reunited. She knew Hezekiah must have a sense of relief that he no longer had to hide away for fear of what people would think.

Soon after everyone had left and Ettie and Elsa-May were done straightening up and about to go home, Ralf and Maddie appeared at the door.

Ralf looked around. "We heard there's a twilight viewing of the house tonight. Is it over already?"

Ettie and Elsa-May looked at each other and smiled.

"No," Elsa-May said. "You're just in time. Come in and take another look around."

CHAPTER 32

The next day, after a good sleep-in and a late, light breakfast, Ettie and Elsa-May sat in their living room.

"What a relief that it's all over with!" Ettie said.

"All things work out in the end. We found Deena's murderer, and Ralf and Maddie are in the process of buying Gabriel's house."

"Do you think they'll make good neighbors?"

Elsa-May shook her head. "They'll be better than some..."

"And worse than others," Ettie finished her sister's sentence with a wry chuckle.

When they heard a car pull up, Ettie stood and looked out the window. "Ah, it's Detective Kelly." Ettie walked over, opened the door and called out, "Is everything all right?"

He got out of the car and gave her a wave. "It is," he called back as he headed toward the house.

"Just in time for breakfast. Would you like some?"

"No thank you. I've just come to—"

"Don't mind Ettie's manners, Detective. Come in and sit down."

Ettie stood back and Kelly passed her and sat down on one of the wooden chairs opposite the couch "I've just come to tell you both that Ryker has been released."

"Ah good. I'd say he would've been pleased about that."

"He was. Mrs. Smith, would you tell me how you found Hezekiah Lapp?"

"Yes. I found the shop name and address from the price stickers on the boxes for Elsa-May's puzzle, and Deena's. The shop was in Hazelton."

"You see, Deena had the same puzzle as me. Exactly the same one."

"We have a lady in our community, Maggie Overberg, and she always knows who's doing what and when they're doing it."

"Or have done it," Elsa-May added.

"So, I asked Maggie if Deena had ever been to Hazelton, Luzerne County and she said she hadn't, at least, not in the last few years. The stickers on the puzzles appeared brand new. They weren't faded and the writing was clear and crisp. Since Gabriel was going to that very township, I asked him to visit the store and see what he could find."

"So, you didn't know Hezekiah was going to be there?"

"No, but I was sure Gabriel would find something."

"And he found Hezekiah there, because he owns the store," Elsa-May said.

Kelly pressed his lips together. "This whole thing would've been solved much quicker if Annie had come forward when she found her."

"She couldn't," Elsa-May said.

Kelly narrowed his eyes at her. "Why not?"

"You see, Annie feared Luke had killed Deena."

"I found that out last night, but that's hardly an excuse."

"Wait a minute, why did she write the note pretending to be Deena?" Elsa-May asked.

"To confuse the timeline, Elsa-May."

"Well, she must've written it after she knew we found Deena."

"She would've," Ettie said. "Would you like a piece of fresh cake, Detective Kelly?"

"Or perhaps try some pickled pears," Elsa-May suggested.

"No thank you, I'm fine."

Elsa-May continued, "She must've written that note in the time between when I told her and after—"

"Yes. I sent you in to tell her about Deena and then you had to go outside and send the ladies on their way," Ettie said. "That's when she would've written the note and concocted her story."

"I see. She was alone and that's when she got the idea to write the note?"

"Exactly. If the day of death was in doubt, then she thought her husband would be safer. Luke was due home, but he stayed on."

"Ah."

Ettie smiled and held up her hands. "So, all I did was discount everything surrounding Annie and what she said, and it became clearer who the murderer was."

Elsa-May shrugged. "If you say so."

"What did you do, Mrs. Smith?" Detective Kelly asked, frowning.

"Think of puzzle pieces as clues. I removed the pieces that belonged elsewhere and then I was able to finish the puzzle with the pieces that belonged."

"Mrs. Smith, I think your whole brain is a puzzle

Ettie chortled.

"But somehow, this time, you put your finger on the problem."

"Also, Annie said she left a note at Deena's house telling her about the quilting bee. There was no note, was there, Detective Kelly?"

"That's one of the reasons I detained her," Detective Kelly told Elsa-May.

"Another thing I can't figure out is Ryker's tire tracks were found at Deena's house and also, Detective

Kelly, you said from Ryker's cell phone records he was near the house on the day she would've died."

"Ryker explained all that while he was in custody. At first, of course, we didn't believe a word of it. He was talking about someone and wouldn't say who it was, so it gave no credibility to his story."

"What was his story?" asked Elsa-May.

"He said that someone he knew called him, upset they'd had an argument with Deena. This person, who he wouldn't name, asked him to drive over to Deena's to see that she was okay. He said he would. The mystery man also asked Ryker to put in a complaint with the telephone company before he left and also to check Deena's horse when he arrived. When you found Hezekiah, all of that fell into place—that it was Hezekiah he was talking about. He wouldn't name him because Hezekiah wanted to remain missing. Ryker respected that even though he personally was facing criminal charges."

Ettie learned forward. "Maybe the apple fell farther from the tree than you first thought."

Kelly chuckled and then rubbed his chin. "I've just realized that myself. Although he was good at telling tall stories about Deena."

Elsa-May said, "I'm so glad Annie wasn't charged with tampering with evidence, or anything."

"She knows she was wrong to do what she did, and she's not likely to reoffend."

Elsa-May looked over at Ettie. "Everyone kept

saying they heard someone in the house, Ettie. Remember?"

"Everyone, Elsa-May, or was it just Annie, trying to throw us off because she thought Luke did it?"

"I see. She was trying to make us think someone else killed Deena and they might've been in the house. You might be right, Ettie."

Detective Kelly laughed.

"What's so funny?"

"The frypan, the pick, and the shovel."

Ettie grimaced.

Detective Kelly said, "You two thought they were murder weapons."

"We heard Ryker's stories about Deena killing Hezekiah with a frypan."

"Yes," Ettie said. "That was one of those pieces that didn't fit the puzzle."

"Poor Deena," Elsa-May said. "I thought the handle fell off the frypan because she hit Hezekiah so hard. It was an odd shape for a frypan, come to think of it."

"Yes, well, we've found the killer and that's another job wrapped up. Thank you both for your help."

"Anytime."

"Oh, and the house next door is sold," Ettie told him. "After you left last night, a couple came through and said they were buying it. It was the same people from the other day."

"They might be quiet neighbors I suspect. They don't look like they'd be rowdy," Elsa-May told him.

He nodded. "That's good to hear. Hopefully, they *will* be good neighbors." He stood up and sighed. "Another day, another pile of paperwork waiting for me."

Ettie and Elsa-May showed him to the door. Then Elsa-May let Snowy out of the bedroom. As usual, Snowy ran about sniffing everywhere Kelly had been, and then he ran to the front door and barked.

"Poor Snowy. He's very fond of Detective Kelly and the detective doesn't even like Snowy."

"Or any animals," Ettie pointed out.

"That's true. Now come into the kitchen, Ettie, for a momentous occasion."

"What is it?"

"You'll see."

Ettie followed Elsa-May to the kitchen leaving Snowy to scratch at the front door. When they walked in, Ettie saw the puzzle was nearly completed. "How did you do this so fast? You've done so much since breakfast."

"I just concentrated, and got it finished way ahead of the recommended timeframe. I want you to be here with me as I place the last of the pieces."

"Go ahead." Ettie sat down and watched Elsa-May as she stood leaning over the puzzle and placing the last pieces.

"Ah. There we go, all done. That last piece was for Deena." Elsa-May then sat down at the table to admire her completed puzzle.

"It is such a nice landscape picture with such pretty greens in the trees."

"It is. You know, Ettie, I can't help thinking whether Deena gave me that puzzle as a clue. She must've known that on the box was a way to lead us to Hezekiah. I mean, she could've taken off the price tag, but she didn't."

"I've been thinking that very same thing."

They both sighed at the exact same time.

"You did well figuring it all out, Ettie."

Ettie pulled her mouth to one side. "I did?"

Elsa-May nodded.

"So, I'm not good for nothing, I'm good for something?"

"That's right, Ettie. You're finally good for something."

Ettie waited a while, and when no negative comment came after that line, she could scarcely believe it. This was perhaps the first real compliment she'd ever gotten from her eldest sister. And, she'd only had to wait eighty odd years to receive it.

Thank you for reading A Puzzling Amish Murder.

THE NEXT BOOK IN THE SERIES

Amish Dead & Breakfast.

Book 24 Amish Dead and Breakfast

In the heart of Amish country lies a quaint bed and breakfast with secrets thicker than a shoo-fly pie. When elderly Amish widow Ettie Smith and her sister are whisked into the world of wedding catering, little did they know their duties would soon expand to investigating a murder.

Before the newlyweds could even churn their marital bliss, the groom ends up deader than last season's corn crop on the library floor. The prime suspect? Thomas, the B&B co-owner, who's forgotten more than just his manners—it seems his memory of the murder has churned into butter.

Add a dollop of suspicious antics in the mix, and

Ettie and her sister find themselves knee-deep in a mystery that threatens to leave a sour taste. Undeterred, they pledge to rise to the occasion, buttering up a grumpy detective as they knead the clues.

In a town known for its simple living, will Ettie churn out the truth behind the groom's death or will the killer continue to roam free, living the cream of the crop life?

If you relish a cozy whodunnit with homespun charm, suspense as thick as homemade jam, and a dollop of humor, you'll love Samantha Price's heartwarming tale.

ABOUT SAMANTHA PRICE

Samantha Price is a USA Today bestselling and Kindle All Stars author of Amish romance books and cozy mysteries. She was raised Brethren and has a deep affinity for the Amish way of life, which she has explored extensively with over a decade of research.

She is mother to two pampered rescue cats, and a very spoiled staffy with separation issues.

www.SamanthaPriceAuthor.com

ETTIE SMITH AMISH MYSTERIES

Book 1 Secrets Come Home
Book 2 Amish Murder
Book 3 Murder in the Amish Bakery
Book 4 Amish Murder Too Close
Book 5 Amish Quilt Shop Mystery
Book 6 Amish Baby Mystery
Book 7 Betrayed
Book 8 Amish False Witness
Book 9 Amish Barn Murders
Book 10 Amish Christmas Mystery
Book 11 The Amish Cat Caper
Book 12 Lost: Amish Mystery
Book 13 Amish Cover-Up
Book 14 The Last Word
Book 15 Old Promises
Book 16 Amish Mystery at Rose Cottage
Book 17 Plain Secrets

Book 18 Fear Thy Neighbor

Book 19 Amish Winter Murder Mystery

Book 20 Amish Scarecrow Murders

Book 21 Threadly Secret

Book 22 Sugar and Spite

Book 23 A Puzzling Amish Murder

Book 24 Amish Dead and Breakfast

Book 25 Amish Mishaps and Murder

Book 26 A Deadly Amish Betrayal

Book 27 Amish Buggy Murder

ALL SAMANTHA PRICE BOOK SERIES

Amish Maids Trilogy

Amish Love Blooms

Amish Misfits

The Amish Bonnet Sisters

Amish Women of Pleasant Valley

Ettie Smith Amish Mysteries

Amish Secret Widows' Society

Expectant Amish Widows

Seven Amish Bachelors

Amish Foster Girls

Amish Brides

Amish Romance Secrets

Amish Christmas Books

Amish Wedding Season